In the Name of God

In the Name of God

PAULA JOLIN

ROARING BROOK PRESS

NEW HILFORD · CONNECTICUT

Copyright 2007 by Paula Jolin
Published by Roaring Brook Press
Roaring Brook Press is a division of Holtzbrinck Publishing Holdings Limited
Partnership
143 West Street, New Milford, Connecticut 06776

Library of Congress Cataloging-in-Publication Data

Jolin, Paula.
In the name of God / Paula Jolin. — 1st ed.
p. cm.
Summary: Determined to follow the laws set down in the Qur'an, seventeen-
year-old Nadia becomes involved in a violent revolutionary movement aimed
at supporting Muslim rule in Syria and opposing the Western politics and
materialism that increasingly affect her family.
ISBN-13: 978-1-59643-211-6
ISBN-10: 1-59643-211-X
1. Muslims—Juvenile fiction. [1. Muslims—Fiction. 2. Family life—Syria—
Fiction. 3. Islamic fundamentalism—Fiction. 4. Syria—Fiction.] I. Title.
PZ7.J662415In 2007
[Fic]—dc22
2006023834

Roaring Brook Press books are available for special promotions and premiums.
For details, contact: Director of Special Markets, Holtzbrinck Publishers.

Book design by Patti Ratchford
Printed in the United States of America
First Edition April 2007

To Um Hamid

# Acknowledgements

Thanks to everyone in the Arab world who offered me a little tea with my sugar, taught me Arabic, and spent hours discussing everything from the Arab Nations Cup to why Syrian men all have facial hair. I learned about Arab culture and politics by watching, listening and paying attention; any mistakes in this book are because I talked too much and didn't listen enough.

My everlasting thanks to Um Hamid and her family – Abu Fouad, Fouad, Hamid, Mohammad, Feras and Shaddi. Also great thanks to the Abdullahi family, especially Amna, Aisha, Hyatt and Fatima (Nooneya).

More thank yous to the people who wanted to change the world with me when we were young: Chris McCarthy Roberts, who started it all, Lucía Muñoz, Chu Kim-Prieto, Nancy Tewksbury and Jiho Huang Bryson.

This book wouldn't have been written if I hadn't learned how to write. Thanks to Ben Tomek, who pushed me to refocus Nadia's story until it was done right, and Andrea Somberg, who believed in my book from the beginning. Thanks to Sandy Smith for her excellent job on the copy edit. Great thanks to the dedicated people at Novelpro, especially founder J. R. Lankford, Lynn Hoffman and James McKinnon. Special thanks to Dave Shields, whose insightful critique made me realize the work had just begun. Thanks also to Dorothy Ray, Brenda Baker, Becky Berg, Dave Damast, Susan Doyle, Angela Germano, Amanda Jenkins, Donna Koppelman, Jamie Lin, Samantha Priestly, Tessa Ropp, Janet Skoog and Jodi Wheeler-Toppen.

Big thanks to my family, who missed me when I disappeared into the Arab world and loved me hard when I came home: my parents, Paul and Virginia Jolin, and my brothers, Gary, Eddie and Tom Jolin. To Julien, who watched a little more Elmo than he should have when I was writing the first draft, and to Maia, who gave me a deadline I couldn't ignore.

Finally, for Mark: I couldn't have done it without you.

# In the Name of God,
## the King,
## the Sovereign Lord

"I love the world after dark," said my cousin Samira as we crossed the main street and entered a narrow, barely-there alleyway. "It's like an enchanted wonderland."

I wouldn't go as far as Samira—I never do—but night does have its promises. That alleyway, for example. By day, a showcase for trash and cracked cement. After dark, a hole in a thousand-year-old castle wall, hinting at fast-moving horses' hooves and secret missions and princesses. Mystery and intrigue. What we found: a pair of scrambling cats, plastic packages crunching under our feet, a less than enticing smell wafting from beside a barrel. Still, Samira said, "It's so quiet and not-Damascus right now. Like we've stepped into the magical world of the jinn or something."

Her sister Yasmine shuddered. "I wish a jinn would come along and offer me a new pair of shoes. My ankles are covered with blisters."

We had been walking for a while. Daoud, another cousin, had arrived at our apartment with a pickup truck and an invitation: "Come and see the city from the top of Qasiyun Mountain. All the tourists go." Mama and Auntie finally gave in to our pleading, and we set off in the back of the truck, Fowzi riding shotgun to protect us.

The view from the mountain was spectacular, all silence and dark cold and winking lights. The city looked less like fifty square miles inhabited by men and industry and more like diamonds in a woman's hair. "That's beauty, Cousin Nadia," said Fowzi, at my elbow. "Interesting, isn't it, that sometimes the things we love are more beautiful from afar?"

He was so close I could smell his cologne, something subtle and foreign my brother had sent him from the Emirates. "Maybe distance gives us perspective," I said. "Or else we're too far away to see all the little flaws."

"And yet God is closer to a man than his jugular vein. And it's God that man loves most."

The mountain breeze whisked over my tightly covered head and I trembled a little. "Fowzi, come and tell us what that building is—the governor's palace or the American Embassy," called Yasmine, and he moved from my side to answer his sister.

All the way home, as I crouched in the corner of the pickup truck, Yasmine and Samira's gossip floated in and out of my ears. "So then she said, 'He's married to me, you know. He shouldn't be giving presents to other girls.' Other girls! Jamila is his *sister*." Blocking out their careless comments, I relived that moment on the mountaintop, wrapped in Fowzi's warm words.

The truck stopped with a sudden screech at the corner of Nazem Pasha Street and Sharia al-Mastaba, interrupting both inner warmth and conversation. Fowzi descended from the cab with a look on his face that suggested an argument. "The truck's broken down," he told us. "Daoud says it could take hours to fix. He's staying here, so we'll have to get a taxi."

"At this time of night?" Samira showed no inclination to move. "Maybe he's exaggerating. What's the problem?"

"We'll never get a cab," said Yasmine.

"Then we'll walk."

Both girls—all right, I admit it, all three of us—squealed in protest. "It must be at least six miles, Fowzi. We can't walk that far. And in heels."

Another point of view: who wears heels to climb a mountain? Not Yasmine, next time. That comment about the jinn bringing her new shoes was hardly the first she'd made. "Enough about your feet," said Samira. "Or I'm going to steal your shoes myself and make you go barefoot."

We came out of the alleyway and onto the main road, lit by a single streetlamp. At the edge of our group, I brushed against a post and bit back a shriek when it moved. Not a post but a young man leaning against a post, hat askew, clothing crumpled. Perhaps I startled him, too, because he began to sing, "Welcome, welcome to the danger zone." I put my hands over my ears.

"Drunk," whispered Yasmine, her eyes widening.

Fowzi stared after the youth as he ambled into the alleyway we'd come from. "I don't know," he said. "Perhaps we should take a different road."

"Don't be stupid," said Samira. "What other road? The longer we walk, the longer we'll have to listen to Yasmine's whining."

We didn't, though. She was silent as we passed through one street and then the next. Fowzi stood at the head of Avenue Sulman, trying to decide whether we would be more likely to find a cab if we went up or around. "Excuse me," said a voice from behind us. Not a drunken voice, one firm with authority. "Identity cards, please."

A young soldier, beret tilted at an angle, casual machine gun at his side, stood outlined by the slender lamplight. "What are you doing out tonight?" he asked. Not suspicious, not friendly, just a question.

No one answered. We girls were busy searching our pocketbooks for our ID cards. Extracting them, we passed them to the soldier, who barely glanced at the pieces of yellow cardboard. "Where's yours?" he asked Fowzi.

"It seems I forgot my wallet."

The soldier was not the only astonished one. No one forgets his wallet. No one leaves home without his identity card. Samira opened her mouth to say something—point out, perhaps, that Fowzi had his wallet at the top of the mountain when he bought us each a Pepsi—but then she closed it again. The soldier, not much older than I, was also at a loss. "I'll have to arrest you," he said at last. "We can't have people wandering the streets without proper identification."

"Can't we vouch for him?" I asked. "You can't leave us, three girls, alone in the street without anyone to watch over us."

The soldier looked at me, and it was a look I didn't like. "Maybe we could take a short walk together," he suggested to my cousin. "Within sight of the young ladies, of course." Fowzi shrugged and the two men headed down the deserted street. The cool winter night encouraged me to huddle deeper into my *manteau*, the protective trench coat I never go anywhere without. Underneath their thin sweaters, my cousins shivered. Yasmine stood up on her toes, freeing her heels from the punishing backs of her shoes. Samira didn't say anything about enchanting wonderlands.

A hundred feet away, the two men were arguing, with vigor but not loud enough to hear. A slip of paper passed between them. Silver. That meant 500 lira—enough to buy Mama a new dress, pay the milkman for months, feast on lamb or chicken every night for a week. I saw Samira swallow. They're almost as poor as we are, for all her father has a job and mine is dead—May God have mercy on his soul—and Samira is a girl who likes pretty things. That five hundred wouldn't go easily.

The soldier had turned the corner and Fowzi almost rejoined us before Samira asked, "What on earth were you thinking?" Fowzi's luck saved him once again. An elusive cab appeared around the corner and slowed to a stop without anyone raising a hand. Fowzi opened the back door and we three girls piled in, silent and circumspect once more.

In the Name of God,
the Light,
the One Who Guides

"He must be terribly poor," said Mama, when Yasmine and Samira had poured out the full story. "These unfortunate boys. The army pays them nothing, and he might have a whole family depending on him for support." Rushing past Fowzi in the cold, we girls had stampeded up the stairs, stumbling over each other as we pushed through the apartment door. Mama, slumped on the couch, opened her eyes quickly enough when Samira proclaimed, "We almost got arrested!" She didn't interrupt though, not even to complain about Fowzi's lack of foresight, which she certainly would have, had my brother Nassir been our escort. I slid out of my *manteau* and let Samira and Yasmine tell the story. To be sure, in their version, Samira wasn't as cold as I remembered, and Yasmine's feet didn't hurt half as much.

"Poor boy?" echoed Samira. "He bilked Fowzi out of 500 lira."

"Where did Fowzi even get 500 lira?" asked Yasmine.

Samira ignored her. "I didn't like the way he stared at us, either."

Mama, looking worried, stood up. "Where is Fowzi now?" she asked.

"Paying off the taxi," said Samira as she flopped down onto the couch. "You know these drivers. He wants triple fare because it's almost midnight, and something more besides—his crippled mother, his exiled brother, et cetera, et cetera."

"I'm going to make some tea," said Mama. "And see what I can find for supper. You must all be starving after your late-night adventure." She moved down the hall toward the kitchen, her sandal-clad feet scuffing against the hardwood floor.

I should have pattered along beside her or even insisted on making the tea myself. My cousins had no such qualms. Samira was searching the couch crevices for something and Yasmine flipped open the cracked case of a plastic compact. "Look at my hair," she said. "Nadia, where do you keep your combs?"

I didn't make my usual comment—*Who are you trying to impress in the middle of the night?*— but pointed her in the direction of the bedroom I share with Mama. When she had disappeared, I wedged myself beside Samira on the couch.

From the kitchen, I heard the clattering of silver trays that meant Mama was trying to extract them from the bottom shelf. "What on earth is going on with Fowzi?" I asked my cousin. Samira shook her rumpled bangs out of her face and leaned past me to reach into the space between the couch and the end cushion. "What do you mean?" she asked. "There's nothing wrong with Fowzi."

"Does he have some kind of death wish? Why in the name of God didn't he show his ID to a man with a gun? And don't tell me he forgot it—Fowzi doesn't forget anything."

Samira tapped her fingers on the denim fabric covering her knee. "Maybe he got fed up with being ordered around all the time."

"That's what you really think?"

"What I really think is that Fowzi left his ID in the pocket of another pair of pants." She bent over and tried to look under the couch. "Do you know where the remote is?"

I stared at her. After-midnight TV consists of raucous music parties from Lebanon and European programs where skinny women prance around in bikinis. Samira wanted to watch that? The same Samira who used to compete with me to see who could recite the most chapters of Qur'an at family gatherings? Who knew the Latin name for every bone in the human body but couldn't tell Queen Latifah from Queen Noor?

"It's probably fallen behind the TV," I told her at last. "But Samira, there's nothing suitable on this time of night."

Mama padded back down the hall, a bowl of orange slices in one hand and a packet of biscuits in the other. "I was watching the loveliest concert," she said, handing the biscuits to Samira and placing the oranges on the table. "Hakim, I think, and some other Egyptian. But that must have finished hours ago."

I couldn't let things go. "You know, Samira, you were complaining about that soldier staring at you tonight—you wouldn't have to worry about that if you wore *hijab*." I raised my hand and adjusted my own scarf, still on my head so I would be covered when Fowzi came in. Which he should have done by now. Before I could start to worry about him, though, Samira said, "I have no intention of wearing a scarf anytime soon," as though she hadn't promised "six more months" at the end of last Ramadan. I knew that argument would go nowhere. "It's God's command," I said instead. "*Say to the Believing Women—*"

"That's all right for old ladies," said Yasmine, reappearing from the depths of the bedroom and helping herself to more than her share of orange slices. "For married women. It makes sense for them, they have husbands. But for us, young girls, it's the time we should enjoy ourselves."

I gaped at her. Mama said gently, "But Yasmine, do you really think God means for you to enjoy yourself by flirting with boys?"

"No, that's not it," said Samira. Maybe she answered because Yasmine's mouth was stuffed with orange, or maybe she's just smarter than her sister. "It's not about boys, or about being young. It's that *hijab* says something about a person, says that she's in a place where she's ready to devote herself to God all the time, and I'm not there yet. I don't want to put it on, and then take it off in a few months because I wasn't ready."

I looked at Samira. Her shiny black hair had been straightened—must have taken her hours—and pulled back with a purple band. She wore makeup these days, not a lot, but her lips were still too red for my taste. She's always been proud of her pale skin and her fine nose and the fact that once, long ago, she got lost in the market and someone mistook her for a foreigner.

"I can only speak for myself," I said, "but wearing *hijab* has helped me to become a person who wants to devote all her time to God. Once you put it on, I don't think you'll want to take it off."

Samira shrugged. In the silence that followed, I heard the kettle whistling in the kitchen. "I'll get it," I said. As I made my way down the hall, Mama launched into a vivid description of the concert. I blocked it out of my head, too caught up in recent events to think about anything else. Samira's defection. Fowzi's odd behavior—where was he anyway? Even the most obstinate taxi driver should have given up by now. Suppose that soldier had followed us home? Or sent his friends? Or worse, his superiors? Maybe the taxi driver was one of the hundreds, thousands—or was it hundreds of thousands?—of people secretly in the pay of the government. A spy in every family, isn't that what they said? Perhaps he'd abducted Fowzi, beaten him up, extracted information from him. Any minute now hobnailed boots might pound up our apartment stairs, angry fists beat against the wooden door.

I shook my head to clear my thoughts. *Don't be ridiculous, Nadia.* As I turned in to the kitchen at the end of the hall, I heard a soft rap on the door behind me.

# In the Name of God,
# the Aware,
# the One Who Knows All Things

No soldier in a green beret, no henchman with a long baton. Just Fowzi, propped against the doorframe in the dim hallway. Of course. How stupid of me. "Fowzi! We thought the earth had opened up and swallowed you."

I moved to let him in and watched as he kicked off his shoes. "Taxi drivers, you know what they're like," he said. "You'd swear this one had driven me to Beijing and back, the fare he wanted to charge. He haggled on and on."

"All this time?" I tossed the ends of my scarf over my shoulder. "I started to worry that your soldier friend might have followed us home."

"I ran into your neighbor," he said. "The one in the last apartment block whose son is studying dentistry. He's worried because the boy seems to know more about cars than teeth."

I leaned against the wall behind me, willing myself to be less suspicious. Was there any reason Fowzi shouldn't have chatted with a neighbor? He certainly wasn't lying about the neighbor's son, who plasters his tooth-decay books with stickers of Mustangs and Z/28s or whatever. I meant to let the moment pass, but I found myself saying, "That incident with the soldier was so strange . . ."

"Of all nights to be stopped by the police," agreed Fowzi. "I had to renew my permit at the Assad Library this afternoon, and when they handed me back my ID card, I stuffed it in the pocket of my backpack. So stupid . . . is that your tea boiling?"

I jumped. I wanted to invite Fowzi into the kitchen with me, to cross-examine him—he was telling the truth, Fowzi always tells the truth, but his statements came off glib, almost rehearsed. Now I sounded like secret police myself. Never mind that; Mama would have a fit if she found me closeted alone with a boy, even Fowzi. Backing into the kitchen, I left him to head off, alone, down the hall.

I turned off the gas and went to the counter, where Mama had set out a silver tray with five empty tea glasses. On tiptoe, I pulled the sugar bowl from the back of the second shelf and plunked it down. One spoon each for me, Samira, and Fowzi; two for Mama; half for Yasmine, who, despite the orange slices, was on a *regime*. I added a sprig of mint to each glass.

Lifting the kettle off the burner, I placed it on the tray and set off for the salon.

As I balanced my way into the hall, I heard Fowzi's voice, raised in anger. Talking about the soldier at last? I quickened my steps.

". . . it isn't right, Auntie, and you know it," he was saying. "They can't pass Auntie Um Noah off on you. They're her sons, they're responsible for her—you're a widow and it's not like you've got a spare room." Not anger, just excitement. How had I forgotten that Fowzi gets excited over everything?

"She's old, she's lonely," said Mama as I came into the room. "I hate to think of her sitting alone in that apartment all day, staring at the walls."

Auntie Um Noah spends her days staring at a color TV, not the walls, thank you very much. Her son and his wife were trying to change her address not because of her loneliness, but all those "I don't mean to interfere but . . ." comments. I didn't say anything, though. Mama knew my opinion on the subject. Old and crotchety, Auntie Um Noah is much too likely to point out the spot on my face or the extra chocolate I tried to sneak for dessert. Or both. *You wouldn't have spots on your face if you didn't eat so much chocolate.* Not very proper or generous or, for that matter, Muslim of me, but I couldn't bear the thought of waking up to her complaints every morning.

I deposited everything in the center of the table. The bottoms of the tea glasses rattled against the silver tray. "I feel sorry for Auntie Um Noah," said Samira. Of course, there was no danger of Auntie moving into their crowded apartment. "Divorced so young, raising twin boys by herself, cooped up in her brother's home for decades."

Fowzi reached for the teapot. "You remember everything, Nadia—tea with mint, my favorite." He passed one glass to Mama and started to pour. "The point is, Auntie, you're too kind, to even think about it. Bassam was saying the exact same thing—"

"You spoke to Bassam?" Mama almost never interrupts people. "Did he say when he'd be back? He's supposed to come home sometime this month."

Fowzi looked surprised. Not surprised, uncomfortable. His dark eyes got bigger as he reached across to collect his tea glass. "Bassam's back already, Auntie. He came two days ago, or was it the day before that? A big surprise. I happened to drop in on Auntie Um Bassam, and you can imagine the uproar."

Samira stretched and yawned. "Pour my tea quick, please, Fowzi. Don't you think we should be getting home?"

"Home?" Mama's face fell. "Aren't you going to stay the night? It's so late and you've already sent the taxi off, it'll take you hours to get another one. You girls can sleep in Nassir's room and the boys can bunk down with blankets on the couch."

Just like that, the conversation changed. The dilemma of Auntie Um Noah, the strange reappearance of Bassam, lost amid the chaos of last-minute sleeping arrangements. And the strange encounter with the soldier? Forgotten under Samira's skillful hands. I poured steaming tea into my cup and took a sip so hot it burned my tongue. Forgotten, but not by me.

PAULA JOLIN

# In the Name of God,
## the Eternal,
## the Independent

"There is no God but God."

Damn. The morning light filtered around my shade, danced across the covers of my bed. I'd missed *fajr*, the morning call to prayer. My bare legs dangled over the side of the bed, my toes shivered on the cold floor, before I realized the phrase hadn't echoed in the low, pious voice of the neighborhood *muezzin*. Not the *muezzin* but Cousin Fowzi, pacing in the room next door.

"Nothing stops them, does it?" he continued. "An old man, confined to his wheelchair, carried by family members to the mosque—that's the enemy of the state of Israel, so dangerous he has to be taken down by missiles?"

I stood up, letting the hem of my nightgown sweep the floor, and reached for my heavy knit robe. My fingers fumbled with a white cotton scarf, dropping it twice before I managed to wrap it around my head. Not bothering to check my appearance in the mirror, I pushed open the door and stepped into the living room.

"Shaykh AbdulHalim?" I asked. Fowzi's words could refer to only one Palestinian leader. "Did something happen to Shaykh AbdulHalim?"

A tousled Nassir sat amid a pile of bunched up blankets on the couch, looking bewildered. Fowzi, washed and dressed, had stopped in front of the TV, arms half raised with some strong emotion.

"What happened?" I asked.

Mama came into the room, her mouth twisted. "Come and

eat," she said to Fowzi, voice so low I had to strain to hear. She looked up and saw me hovering in the doorway. "Did you pray yet, Nadia? You don't want to be late for school."

"I'm not hungry, Auntie," said Fowzi. "And speaking of late, the girls have to get all the way out to Harasta." He was already talking loud enough, he didn't need to raise his voice. "Samira? Yasmine? Put away your pocket combs or whatever and let's go." He turned back to Nassir. "Do they think that killing Shaykh AbdulHalim will stop the suicide bombers? No. It will not. We will bring a thousand bombers, a million bombers, whatever it takes, until they treat us with respect, not like wild dogs who have peed in their backyard. And if they say they will kill ten of us for every one we kill—I say, the Muslim Nation is a billion people strong."

His angry words echoed in the air. "Fowzi." I almost reached out and caught his arm. "You don't have to yell at us. We're not the enemy."

"Of course not." He raked his hands through his cropped hair. Fowzi had been a beanpole as long as I could remember, with ill-fitting clothes and a straggly beard. When did he grow into his tall frame, still slim but strong and supple? When had his beard filled out? "I know who the enemy is."

Israel, of course. Stealing Palestinian land more than fifty years ago wasn't enough for them, they have to persecute the people who are only struggling to get their own back. The United States of America, enemy number 2. The Arab countries could have shaken Israel into the sea with the effort of a camel swishing its tail if it weren't for American money and guns. But Fowzi's next comment took me by surprise: "I blame our governments as much as anyone. Where is the Egyptian army? Where is Jordan? Where are all the mercenary marching men Saudi Arabia's billions could hire? Where is Syria? Is this a Muslim country, or is it not? I say not. And all who recognize that should join together in calling for retribution." His final words were almost a prayer. "Death to the oppressors of the Muslims—smite the Unbelievers, oh Lord."

It wasn't that I didn't agree with him. But nobody says things like that. Nobody takes the risk. I couldn't help admiring his outspoken words even as I glanced around the room to make sure the damage was minimal. Doors locked tight, windows still shut against the evening cold. No strangers present—only Mama with her worried frown, Nassir with his bedhead, Samira clipping earrings in place as she emerged from the bathroom, Yasmine poking her head out of the bedroom, one plump cheek pressed against the doorjamb.

Still, I gave a sigh of relief when Mama interrupted the silence to say, "Come, you've got to eat before you go. No objections, Fowzi."

It was Yasmine who objected. "I never have breakfast."

Samira picked up her purse off the back of the armchair but didn't add anything. Was she upset about Shaykh AbdulHalim or worried that her blue earrings didn't match her striped blouse? I couldn't tell.

"Auntie, you're too kind," said Fowzi. "We'll grab something when we get home."

"I'll make each of you a falafel sandwich to take on the bus." Mama moved aside and herded my cousins down the hall. Behind her, images flickered across a muted al Jazeera as a single-story wooden building blew up again and again. "Nadia?" Mama's voice was sharper than usual. "You have just enough time to say your prayers before school if you hurry now." She turned and disappeared after the others.

Though I knew she was right, I stared blindly at the TV for a few minutes. Not weeping silent tears over the shaykh's tragic death or asking God to come to the aid of the Muslims. No, I was remembering a hot summer day a few years ago, and Mama making falafel sandwiches for four boys—Nassir, Mohammad, Bassam, and Fowzi—who planned to take the bus to Mezzah and apply for cards at Assad Library. "They're good for exactly four years," Nassir told us when he passed his around the table that evening. Exactly. Which meant they should have been renewed on a hot summer day, not a breezy spring afternoon.

"You want to move out of the way?" growled Nassir. "Aren't you supposed to be getting ready?"

I moved. Out of the way and back to my room. But I was still staring blindly.

# In the Name of God,
## the Watcher,
## the Watchful

I've always been a religious girl, prayed and fasted, and when the time was right, told Mama I was ready to wear a scarf. I've never been the kind of girl who sneaks around with boys, and I tried a cigarette only once, at age eight, on a dare from Samira. Small sins, though, they're like a thousand tiny chinks in the plate armor of my piety: unkind gossip, stubbornness, lazing on the couch when I could be helping Mama. How can I, how can any of us, expect to be rewarded in our struggle against the Unbelievers when we fail the struggle with our own conscience?

I doubt I was the only one thinking about struggle as I made my way home from school in the afternoon. Young men mourning Shaykh AbdulHalim packed the streets, feet pounding as they tramped along together, shouting out their disdain for murder. I avoided the main thoroughfares; packs of angry men are hardly the safest setting for a proper young girl. Plenty of boys are respectable, of course, it's only the ones with the greedy eyes, the wandering fingers, that you have to watch out for. I checked to be sure that my scarf was secure, my *manteau* safeguarding me against the blowing wind.

I didn't mind taking the long route home. I wasn't eager to get there, to Mama's weeping and Nassir's anger and the neighbors' stone-lipped silence. Israel deserved these things, of course, but it was not Israel who had to suffer them.

I crossed a deserted side street and caught a glimpse of marching boots through a gap between the buildings. *"Allahu*

*Akbar!*" they chanted. "Death to the Oppressors of the Muslims. Smite the Unbelievers, oh Lord."

*Death to the Oppressors, smite the Unbelievers.* That was Fowzi's slogan. I left the sidewalk, trudged through the dusty gravel, and headed straight for that gap. I'd done my best all day not to think about Fowzi—his strange behavior with an armed soldier, the unexplained lie about his library card, what was all that to me?

My heart beat faster as I darted between the pair of buildings, a doctor's office on one side, a pharmacy on the other. Was this a revolution? Would I find Fowzi, fist raised in defiance, leading a frenzied crowd?

Crammed shoulder to shoulder, ten or twelve across, the men surged down the paved avenue. Young professionals wearing business suits marched side by side with teenagers in ill-fitting jeans and ragged T-shirts. Underage boys weaved in and out of the mass of men. Here and there a gold cross sparkled in the sunlight; Arab Christians, out in solidarity with our cause. All shouted the same sentence, "Death to the Oppressors," again and again. The phrase had even been scrawled in black ink on white canvas and raised above the heads of the crowd.

My pounding heart began to thud. A revolution—the Muslims rising up against their powerful overlords to restore the rule of God at last. *Get out of here, Nadia. Turn, return the way you came, don't look back. This is no place for a girl.* I continued to scan the crowd for Fowzi, a glimpse of his neatly trimmed beard, his fervent brown eyes.

A faint whirring sound echoed under the roar of the crowd and I turned my head to find its source. My heart stopped, my pride in Fowzi quailed. About fifty meters behind me, a dull green jeep pulled up to a stop sign and screeched to a halt. Half a dozen soldiers dismounted, machine guns strapped to their shoulders, wooden batons gripped in their clenched fists.

Unbidden, I remembered Hama, the pious city in central Syria where President Assad's father had attacked his own citizens before I was born. Besieged them and bombed them because a few Muslims had dared to argue for an Islamic state. Thirty thousand people wound up dead. Then I remembered Fowzi, tearing across the playground after me the day I left my coat on the swing, reciting Qur'an to us little kids when we were too young to read, buying Samira and me so many Popsicles one Friday that our lips turned blue. *Run, Nadia* warred with *Save Fowzi* and this time I knew why my feet wouldn't move.

The soldier seemed to have no such problem. His broad body was beside me, blocking out the sun. I stared hard at the ground. Would he know I was related to the ringleader? Was there still time—somehow—to save Mama, Nassir, the girls?

"You'd better move along," said the soldier in the ugly accent of the southeast, Deir Ezzor or some other barbaric town. "This is no place for a girl."

My eyes flew upward. His gun remained flat against his shoulder, his baton wasn't aimed at my head. "Death to the Oppressors of the Muslims," chanted the crowd. "Death to Israel, death to America." They weren't talking about the government after all. My panic receded but I still felt fuzzy-brained, one of those girls who can solve quadratic equations but gets lost two blocks from home.

The soldier hadn't moved. He lowered his voice. "Unless you're looking for a little excitement? I finish at six, and I know a place . . ."

Unbelievable. A respectable *hijabi* girl lingers with her thoughts for a minute and he takes it as an invitation. Under other circumstances, I might have slapped him, but I contented myself with a dirty look and turned away.

What was the matter with me? Seeing soldiers, war, and death everywhere. I'm not one of those girls with a runaway imagination—well, all right, I am, but I have it well under control. Not like Yasmine, thinking that every well-dressed boy who sees her on a street corner is going to rush to ask her father for her hand in marriage. I'm sensible, grounded-in-reality Nadia, who says her prayers five times a day and studies until she dreams in scientific notation.

I shook my head. I didn't want to puzzle over Fowzi or relive my second close encounter with a soldier in two days or agonize over Shaykh AbdulHalim. Recite Qur'an? Every verse I could think of seemed to involve smiting the Unbelievers.

Caught up in not thinking, I almost tripped over the beggar whose usual haunts include the corner before our apartment building. I offered him a smile and the fifty lira at the bottom of my backpack. Like all the best charity, it pinched. I'd meant to put that fifty lira toward new shoes. Then again, I had working feet to put in my old shoes, unlike the beggar, who had neither. *And spend in charity, for whatever good deed you do, you shall find it with God.*

Satisfied that I'd found a verse that had nothing to do with smiting, I scampered up the stairs of our building and slammed the door behind me. In the living room, Nassir was arguing with the referee on television—something about a foul and a penalty kick.

"Nadia," Mama said, and she sounded cold. "I want to speak with you for a minute. Come to the kitchen, please."

Nassir's voice reached opera level. "But he was totally legit, he got the ball, he played the ball!"

I entered our tiny kitchen. The afternoon sun shone through the single window on the west wall and Mama had turned on the overhead lamp as well. A large bowl filled with water and peeled potatoes waited on the countertop. Two pots hummed on the stove and a pan sizzled, cooking meat. "Nadia," said my mother. "Where have you been?"

My eyes flew to her face. I couldn't understand her anger. "It took me a while to get home because there were mourners everywhere," I said. "I had to take a detour."

"I see."

"What?"

Her eyes held mine, strong and steady. "From now on, please let me know when you're going to be late, Nadia. The other girls in your class from this building came home at least ten minutes ago. Why didn't you walk with them?"

"I stayed after school a few minutes to discuss something with Miss. A few minutes. You can't possibly think I was doing something improper? Something forbidden?"

Mama sighed. "I didn't say that. I didn't say that people gossip and that a woman's most important asset is her reputation, but you know it anyway. Take this as a warning, please, and next time, don't be late." She turned back to the stove and stirred something in the closest pot.

A minute passed, the only conversation carried on by the simmering meat. Then Mama said, her voice still distant, "You might want to finish your lessons tonight. Auntie Um Bassam's having a party tomorrow, a welcome-home bash for Bassam. She especially asked for you."

What was this, a royal command? "Mama! Bassam's been home how long now? And he hasn't even been to see you. As though he wasn't your favorite nephew but any old Mohammad or Ahmad or Omar. Think of all those days you made him sandwiches so he wouldn't have to study on an empty stomach." I stopped the angry words bubbling up and stomped across to sit at the table. There's nothing wrong with Bassam, really, except that he's not religious enough for me.

Mama stirred the pot again. "Auntie said he's brought me some of that chocolate, the kind we had the last time, with the gooey centers, from Belgium, I think, or *Swisra*." She knew exactly what I was thinking: *Chocolate, what kind of gift is that?* Not that I cared about myself—

*Be honest, Nadia.* I did care about myself, at least a bit. Last time Bassam came home, he arrived at our house the second night, arms laden with packages done up in brightly colored wrapping paper, like foreigners do for their birthdays. He brought me a gold necklace with a pendant of a crescent moon—"Because your eyes light up like the night stars, Cousin."

Mama was still not looking at me. "Maybe Bassam is saving up for marriage or something," she said. "Auntie said he told her even if all the other cousins come, it won't be a party without you there."

Mama didn't have to be so subtle. I knew she hoped for a match between Bassam and me, but I wanted a pious husband, not a rich one. I opened my mouth to rattle off the school assignments I had to complete over the weekend when Mama's words sank in. *All the other cousins.* Fowzi would be there. Under cover of the festive atmosphere I could—not interrogate him, that wouldn't be right, but ask him a few simple questions. Bring up the slogan, for example. Even if it wasn't a revolution, there was something going on, something I didn't understand. How did Fowzi get that whole crowd to march to the beat of his words? Making my voice casual as I traced a pattern on the plastic tablecloth, I said, "Auntie Um Fowzi and her family will be there?"

Mama took the bait. "Can you see Yasmine missing a party?" She clicked her tongue—at Yasmine for her party-loving ways, or at herself for giving in to the urge to gossip? Then she caught the handle of the front pot with the wide sleeve of her *galabiya* and nudged it to the back burner. "Samira will be there too, but not Fowzi. He's going to Aleppo."

Aleppo? My finger stilled at the corner of the table. What kind of intrigue was he up to there? I pictured him in the back of a donkey cart, its young driver urging the animal through the narrow streets of the covered market. Fowzi's face is intent, his hands grip the cart tightly, his hoarse voice whispers, "Faster—faster."

Maybe my imagination is not as under control as I thought.

". . . his boss at the construction site wants to order some more supplies and the only one he trusts to do it is Fowzi."

My chair scraped against the linoleum floor with an irate

murmur as I pushed it back. "Doesn't matter to me. I have too many lessons to go to the party anyway."

"You can do your lessons in the early afternoon." Mama, gentlest of souls, is a brick wall when it comes to family responsibilities. "I'll send Nassir back for you in the evening."

I didn't argue further. When she asked me to chop the vegetables for the *fatoush* salad, I flung open the refrigerator door, moved aside the leftovers, and found three cucumbers pressed up against the back wall. I pulled them out, returned to the table, and began chopping.

# In the Name of God,
## the Patient

Nassir had to ring Auntie's doorbell twice before anyone heard us. No surprise, since boisterous music seeped through the cracks around the door. The second time, he leaned against the bell with his shoulder and stayed there, until one voice seemed to rise above the rest. "A minute, a minute . . . are you mad, pressing the bell like that?"

Samira opened the door as though she were married and it was her own apartment. She wore a pink dress with a neckline I wouldn't let my mirror see me in, and a gold necklace to make sure no one missed it. "Cousin," she said. "I couldn't believe it when they told me you were missing the party to do lessons. I knew there had to be some mistake." If she'd had a cigarette, she would have blown smoke in my face.

Before she joined the glamour girl crowd, Samira and I shared each other's every secret. She was going to marry one of my brothers and we would each have baby boys who would grow up to be best friends. We'd bonded in primary school, when it took the two of us to keep a screaming Yasmine from stepping on a wet and bedraggled spider.

A mutual interest in bugs went a long way. Bugs reminded me that the tiniest thing God creates is perfect. Samira is obsessed with scientific accuracy. We even wrote a book together, *Insects We Have Known*, by Nadia and Samira. Pictures of every bug in Damascus crawled across the pages, accompanied by the scientific information we copied out of her father's encyclopedia.

Best friends, until the morning Samira woke up and decided she was more interested in hairspray than hornets, lipstick than lizards.

"I was doing my lessons, Samira," I said when the imaginary smoke cleared. "It's just that I'm finished now." Someone from the salon shouted her name and she spun around, calling, "Coming!" Nassir was already greeting a handful of twentysomething boy cousins with cheek kisses and comments about football. I shook hands all around and made my way into the salon.

Sofas lined three walls and the kitchen table had been set up in the center of the room, covered with cake and soft drinks. People were everywhere that furniture wasn't. Mama sat ensconced on the nearest couch, pinned into place by a trio of aunts; uncles clustered in front of the corner TV and shouted about politics. Boy cousins and girl cousins stood in separate groups, detaching themselves now and again to cut pieces of cake for the older generation.

"Nadia!" Bassam intercepted me, broader than I remembered him, stouter around the waist. Too many McDonald's lunches in the Emirates. "I've been calling you since you came in—didn't you hear me? Thanks for coming."

"Praise God for your well-being," I said, grateful that Arabic has a rote expression for everything. Yasmine joined us before I had to say anything else, a sloshing Coke in one hand.

"May God keep you well," said Bassam. "You look fantastic—better than your pictures." I flushed. I knew that my brother Mohammad, who lived down the street from Bassam in the Emirates, shared everything with him, but I didn't like being reminded of it. Bassam should have remembered that communication goes both ways. His secret Filipina girlfriend was not much of a secret anymore. "It's not like he's going to marry her, Mama," Mohammad scoffed when she got upset over the news. "Think of it more like a language course. Filipinas are great for learning English."

Recalling this, I pressed my lips together. No one noticed though, because Yasmine said, "Did you hear Bassam's big news? He's moving to America."

"What?"

Bassam stuck both hands in the pockets of his khaki pants. "Not exactly. There's a chance—my boss's friend from university has his own company, and they're looking for someone with exactly my *skill set*." I hate when people insert English into their conversation, especially when I don't understand it. "If they can get me a visa, well, then they'll offer me a job. No promises yet."

More than Bassam's weight had changed. His white shirt, stiffened with starch, was thick and expensive-looking. His mustache had sprouted from the sparse pine-needle look into a full-grown bush. And his eyes—were they shifty? "Bassam, you wouldn't really move there, would you? Not when they're attacking Muslims in Iraq? When they're all that stands between Israel and the sea?"

Bassam seized on my last sentence. "Can you believe Israel, what happened to Shaykh AbdulHalim? Don't these people ever think about the wrath of God?"

I had plenty to say about the wrath of God, but over Yasmine's shoulder, I saw Mama beckon me. "I'll be right back," I told them. Or not. I crossed the room, shaking hands with Samira's father and swapping cheeks with three girl cousins from the suburbs before I reached Mama.

She was trapped between Auntie Um Suheil and the edge of the couch. Auntie Um Suheil, my father's cousin, our downstairs neighbor and a blue-ribbon busybody, led a riotous argument with Fowzi's mother and grouchy Auntie Um Noah about which shop sells the cheapest fabric. My face flushed at the sight of Auntie Um Noah, and I couldn't help hoping Mama hadn't issued her "Please come live with us" invitation yet.

"I'm glad I made you come," Mama said, motioning me to pull up a chair. "All day it worried me, you home alone." She smoothed her skirt over the tops of her legs. "On another topic, are you being polite to Bassam?"

"Mama!"

"Nadia's nice to everybody," said a voice from behind me. I

would have thought Mama too old to blush. To be fair, Fowzi wasn't supposed to be here at all.

I stood up slowly and turned toward him. "You didn't go to Aleppo then?" I asked.

Mama and the aunties managed to dislodge themselves from the couch, and they were all asking the same question. "I missed the train," said Fowzi as he made his way around the room, shaking hands with the women and kissing the men on the cheeks. "Then I spent the whole afternoon trying to track down my boss to see how much trouble I was in. When I finally found him, he said, 'Did I tell you to go to Aleppo?'"

Everyone laughed as we resumed our seats. Fowzi ended up in the center of the room with Yasmine and Bassam, and I ended up with Auntie Um Suheil. "How are your studies going?" she asked me.

"Uh, fine."

"Nadia's hoping to pass into medicine," she told the whole room, although no one was listening. "It'll be interesting when you and Samira take your baccalaureate exams next year, to see who scores higher." Not a nice thing to say, since Samira always scores higher than I do.

"Samira should do very well," I said. I didn't admit it to Auntie Um Suheil, but it drives me crazy that Samira, her hair sprayed in place and her eyes and mouth outlined in sticky goo, always gets the answer right.

"You're a smart girl too, Nadia. Look at this afternoon, almost missing a welcome-home party to get your lessons done."

Yasmine's laughter floated out over the music and the TV. I willed myself not to turn around. There were so many things I needed to ask Fowzi, serious things, about the marchers and the government and the future. The world was falling apart and all Yasmine could do was laugh?

I turned around. Yasmine stood in the center of the room, surrounded by Samira and a handful of other girl cousins. Bassam had been co-opted into a conversation with his father and three uncles, and Fowzi was nowhere to be seen.

"Excuse me, Auntie," I said. "I'm going to get a glass of water."

I slipped through the crowd without anyone much noticing me. Turned the corner, peeked into the kitchen—no Fowzi there. Opened the apartment door—no Fowzi smoking illicitly in the hall. (Not that he *would* but . . . ) Walked past the salon, scanned the back bedroom—no beanpole Fowzi head and shoulders above the children arguing over comic books. I headed back to the salon, and was hit by the bathroom door when Fowzi opened it and stepped out.

"Nadia! I am so sorry—I had no idea you were there. Do you, uh, need to—"

I ignored his embarrassment. "I need to talk to you, Fowzi."

Had everyone changed overnight? Unlike Bassam, whose Gulf salary had transformed him into a glossy picture in a magazine, Fowzi had changed on the inside. Stronger somehow, more confident, a better Muslim. He wasn't going around in a flowing *galabiya* with a white prayer cap on his head, passing beads between his fingers at every moment. No, Fowzi, in his worn but pressed jeans and his button-down striped shirt, looked the same but was not the same old Fowzi at all.

"Something to do with your studies?"

What did I say now? I took a deep breath. He smelled like soap and deodorant and crisp early spring afternoons. "I can't stop thinking about what you said the other day. About how things have to change. And I agree with you—"

Fowzi wasn't looking at me. "Nadia," he said. "This is hardly the place to talk about that. I went too far. I was upset about Shaykh AbdulHalim—understandable, I think."

"You're shutting me out again," I said.

He looked at me now. I'd never paid attention to his eyes before, just dismissed them as boring brown. I'd never noticed the dark flecks that gave them surprising depth. "I'm not shutting you out, Nadia. And I wasn't before. Don't invent some imaginary scenario, where you see me—or yourself—as some romantic figure. Trust me, it's not worth it."

"I didn't say anything about romance."

He placed his hand on the back of his neck. "Not that kind of romance. I meant intrigue and danger and—you know what I mean. I'm not going to be more specific in the middle of a party where anyone could overhear."

"But Fowzi, the protests yesterday, they were using your slogan. 'Smite the Unbelievers, oh God.'"

Shifting from one foot to the other, he said, "Simple explanation. I'm the one who copied that slogan—it was all over TV." That was that. Or was there a moment of hesitation before he came out with the answer? Was I going crazy?

"Come into the salon, Nadia, let's see what my sisters are up to."

I trailed Fowzi as he walked down Auntie Um Bassam's short hallway. What was wrong with me? I'd chased him around the house and cornered him in front of the bathroom and whispered alone with a boy in the hall. This was glamour-girl attitude, not the behavior of a respectable *hijabi*. It wasn't as if I was in love with him. Fowzi wasn't my type. Too skinny and too tall and too serious. Then again, serious times called for serious people. And I couldn't ignore his intriguing eyes and handsome beard and the fact that he smelled like a man, not a fashion model. He was righteous and striving to be a better Muslim every day—what more could a good Muslim girl ask for in a husband?

Was I in love with Fowzi after all?

# In the Name of God,
## the Perceiver,
## the Finder

"We're not staying long," said Yasmine as she and Samira popped in the door a few afternoons later. "Not even taking our coats off. I need new shoes and Mama finally found the money for them, so we're on our way down to the markets in Salheya."

"You won't have a cup of tea?" asked Mama. "Nadia, your cousins are here." I poked my head around the kitchen door. "Oh, there you are."

"Do you have too much studying to do?" Samira asked me. "Or would you like to come with us? We'll probably be forever, though, because you know Yasmine, she has to stick her foot in every shoe before she finds one she likes."

I'd been inventing and discarding strategies for unlocking the puzzle of Fowzi's mysterious behavior ever since the party. Interrogating Samira seemed as good a starting point as any. "I'll come," I said. "Let me get dressed properly."

Yasmine stared but Samira covered her rudeness. "Excellent," she said. "No, really, Auntie, no tea. We'll wait for you downstairs then, Nadia."

"I'm glad you're going with them," Mama said to me after they left. "You could be such a good influence. And they're not bad girls. Only a little exuberant."

I wondered if she would have called it exuberant ten minutes later, when Yasmine told the taxi driver to head to Mukhayyam al Yarmuk. Not Salheya, where all the best shops are located, but a Palestinian refugee camp. Mukhayyam al Yarmuk isn't the kind of refugee camp you see on TV, out in the desert, surrounded by barbed wire. It's part of Damascus, and there are shops and buildings and markets. But the majority of Syria's three million Palestinians live there, and—true or exaggerated—it's rumored to be soaked in violence. No terrorist acts, just a lot of people who can't get along. Midnight knifings, loud fistfights in the afternoon, honor killings.

The Palestinians get a bad rap all the way around.

Still, I wasn't allowed to go there. I was so not allowed to go there, no one had ever bothered to forbid it. "Are you crazy?" I asked Yasmine as the driver put the car in gear and skittered into a tiny gap in the oncoming traffic. The car behind us shrieked to a stop and the smell of burning rubber floated through the half-open front window before our driver peeled away. "What on earth do you want with Yarmuk?" A cold breeze whipped through the window and fluttered the ends of my scarf.

My cousins exchanged glances. "We can't afford anything in Salheya," said Samira. "If you must know. You can buy the exact same thing in the markets in Yarmuk for a fraction of the price."

"If I must know? Excuse me? I'm in the car with you, driving to a place I'd never want to go, so—uh—I think it's a little bit my business."

The taxi driver looked over his shoulder as he took a sharp right turn. I would have rather he looked at the road. "You girls still want to go to Yarmuk? I can take you to Salheya if you want."

One thing Syrians do very well is mind each other's business. Samira shot the driver a dirty look. "We said Yarmuk."

"There's nothing wrong with Yarmuk," said Yasmine. "It's exactly like everywhere else. And they have excellent prices, and a much better selection than Salheya or Muhajireen. The shopkeepers start lower, plus you can bargain them down."

"You're the one who's supposed to be so sympathetic to the Palestinian cause," said Samira to me. "Don't you think that supporting their industry would help more than ranting about their plight to people who already agree with you?"

I gripped the armrest as the taxi roared around a corner. "Their industry? You think the stuff they sell in Yarmuk was produced in Palestine, by Palestinians?"

"No. But I think that the Palestinians who live here are not treated very well—they came with nothing, they've had to build everything from scratch, they don't even have citizenship—so I think that buying things from their shops is a way to help their economy. Here. In Syria. Where they live." Samira leaned back against the seat. "And if the prices happen to be cheaper, well, that benefits both of us."

I stared at my cousin. The taxi driver said, "You girls shouldn't be going to Yarmuk alone, you know. It's not safe. I'm undecided, but I'm thinking to take you back to your parents. Next time, you'll think twice before you disobey them."

Samira looked up and met my eyes. So many things I'd never noticed about my cousin were written clearly across her face: stubbornness and cleverness and pride. I felt foolish and alone, and unsure of what to do. I could, probably should, ask the driver to stop the car, then get out and take a bus back. Then I'd have to tell Mama what happened. The repercussions on Samira and Yasmine would be fierce—they might not be allowed out alone again, not till they were married—and they would think I was a terrible prig.

And I'd never find out what Fowzi was up to.

My other option: ride with them to Yarmuk. Get out, keep an eye on them. I would have to hide it from Mama, but with care, I wouldn't tell any lies.

The driver pulled onto the straight stretch of road that led to the refugee camp. We didn't speak again since he'd made it clear that if we did, we'd be listening to his opinion. Careless of our comfort, he rolled his window all the way down and raised the volume on the radio. "Three Palestinian youth were killed today when an Israeli soldier opened fire on them as they exited a taxi in Ramallah," said the announcer. "Two youths died instantly while the third, inflicted with bullet wounds in the upper arms and chest, was left upon the ground. Unable to get an ambulance through the Israeli barricade, the youth died in his mother's arms . . ."

Yarmuk. As Yasmine leaned forward and argued with the driver about the fare, I peered through the window until Samira pushed me from the car, sending my feet into a puddle of cold water. The sun had snuck behind a cloud and the unpaved streets of Yarmuk stared back at us, dreary and dirty in the afternoon cold. "Samira," I whispered. "Is this about a boy?"

I caught a fraction of a pause before she tossed her head. "You're like a middle-aged woman, Nadia," she said. "You should lighten up. You know what? It's possible to be young and have fun and even do some things that are unacceptable in our society without transgressing the laws of God."

Yasmine looked pleased with herself as she emerged from negotiations with the cursing taxi driver. We crossed the street together. The open stalls were built one beside the other and crowds of people clustered around the bins at the front. The muddy streets didn't seem to bother Samira and Yasmine, who both wore jeans, but the cold muck stung as it soaked through the thin stockings that covered my ankles.

Single file, we passed the produce section, stands piled high with bananas and mouthwatering oranges; the butcher shops, awnings dangling with fresh meat; and a couple of commercial shops, walls lined with foil packages of biscuits. Samira, in the lead, seemed to know exactly where she was going. She took a sharp right and we trudged behind her down a narrow alley. Barricaded doors and windows faced us. I shivered. Hard to believe it, but people lived here.

We came out on a larger road, another portion of the market. These stalls were multicolored and more cheerful, if not cleaner. T-shirts every hue of the rainbow hung from the sides of the first stall. At the second, an enormous bin held shoes. "There," said Samira. "I told you they'd have them."

Yasmine let out a squeal.

"Relax," said Samira as her sister squeezed between two older women in enveloping black *abayas*. "The shoes aren't going anywhere without you."

I tilted my head and looked at her. "How did you know about this place?"

She shrugged. "Came here with Mama once." She met my skepticism with bright eyes. "She buys her gold here. Cheaper than Midan or Salheya."

Not surprisingly, Yasmine didn't find the shoes she wanted at the first shop. Nor the second or third. As I trailed her down the Yarmuk shoe district, my thoughts wandered. Maybe Samira was right, we weren't doing anything wrong. Maybe it was just Mama's prejudice that deemed Salheya a safe place and Yarmuk a dangerous one. I respected her desire to protect me, of course. But there had to be a balance between the American "let them live free and die" and the Saudi "wrap them in Velcro and stick them to the inside of the house."

Caught up in my own thoughts, I wasn't paying much attention to what was going on around me. If I hadn't turned sideways to let two men on bicycles pass by, I would have missed him entirely. He was slim and dark, straight black hair pushed back over his ears. Clean-shaven and not my type. He didn't take his eyes off us—Yasmine rummaging through piles of shoes, Samira staring around with that haughty lift to her shoulders, me . . . me, awkward and out of place.

"Who's he?" I asked.

"Who's who?"

"That boy over there. The one staring at us."

"I can't help it if people stare," said Samira. "That's all boys do in this country. Stare and hiss, as though any girl's going to pay attention to someone who sounds like a snake."

He stepped off the curb with a sudden lurch. Not drunk, not in the middle of the afternoon. Still, something about him reminded me of the man we saw the night Fowzi almost got arrested.

Not the soldier, before that; the man singing the filthy song about, yes, about danger. And danger, in the form of a half-grown boy with a killing machine, was what we'd found. Not that I thought it was the same man. In a city of three million people, there must be thousands of young men who looked and walked like that.

"Stop staring," Samira hissed. "You're making it worse. Ignore him."

I tore my eyes away. When I looked back, he had crossed the packed streets and disappeared into the crowd. No, not disappeared. There he was again, his dark head reappearing among the heads bobbing in and out of the shops. Reappearing, and heading straight toward me.

# In the Name of God,
## the Incomparable

A crash erupted behind us. I whipped my head around to find the bin toppled over, shoes spilling onto the ground, and Yasmine holding a pair of glittery green heels high above her head. "At the bottom of the barrel," she said, ignoring the squawking shop boy as he demanded she help him clean up the mess.

I turned back to the street and scoured the crowd, but my dark-haired starer had vanished. Had Yasmine's outburst scared him off? Or had he been heading for some narrow side street in the first place?

"Do you know that guy or something?" asked Samira.

"Of course not." I tore my eyes from the chaotic street scene to look at her. "I thought you did."

Samira opened her purse and began rooting through it. "I'm not the one who couldn't take my eyes off him." That was ridiculous. And not worthy of discussing.

"Samira, I meant to ask you—well, ask both of you. . ." I cast my eyes to Yasmine, who was offering two bills to the angry shop boy. He ignored them, pointing and waving at the shoes in the mud. If he knew Yasmine as well as I did, he'd know he was wasting his time. "It's about Fowzi. I admire his commitment to religion so much. I wondered, he seems to have so much influence, I mean, I wondered if he's ever thought about teaching religion."

A pack of young married women with babies swarmed around us, jostling Samira, but she didn't look up from her pocketbook. "I don't think teaching's something Fowzi wants to do," she said. "But you'd have to ask him that." She brought her hand out of her purse and stared hard at a broken nail. "If you're looking for someone to give you lessons in fanaticism, you'll have to look elsewhere."

Not very polite in my surprise, I stared at her. I meant to say, "Who, me, a fanatic?" and laugh. What actually came out was, "Why are people always so down on fanatics? Fanatic in devotion to God, we're all supposed to be that. Fanatical students, fanatic in loyalty to our families. I hate the way people use *fanatic* as though it's a dirty word."

She stuffed the hand with the broken nail in the pocket of her jeans. "You've changed so much, Nadia," she said. Then she turned and grabbed her sister by the elbow. "You've got your shoes, let's go."

When Samira and Yasmine claimed that they had to stop at "one more store, for pencils," I let them go and took the taxi home alone. As I opened the door of our apartment, I heard a rustling of papers in the other room, and someone saying, "... but isn't that banned in Syria?"

The men in the salon hadn't turned on the lights or the TV. From my position in the hallway, it looked almost as though they were lounging around a dark cave. Nassir lay sprawled out on the sofa, Bassam sat upright in an armchair, and Fowzi knelt on the floor, bent over the coffee table. When he saw me, he swept a cheaply bound blue paperback off the table and shoved it into the small leather briefcase beside his knees. He clicked the case shut, then greeted me. "*Salaam aleikum*, Cousin." *Peace be with you.*

"*Aleikum salaam.*" Was my heart beating faster or did I just think it should be? "Where's Mama?"

Nassir jerked a finger in the direction of the bedroom. "On the phone." I looked around the room. Mama must have made the boys a snack: plates littered with cake crumbs and dirty forks lined the edge of the table and empty tea glasses graced the silver tray in the center. I knew I should carry them out to the kitchen, but I had another priority: getting a look at that blue book. "So, what were you guys talking about?"

"Football," said Nassir.

Since when did the government ban players' manuals? Before I could ask, Mama appeared in the doorway. "Nadia," she said, "I think there's tea left if you want it."

She'd been crying. She had washed her face, but her eyes betrayed her. Or maybe it's just that I know her so well. Of all the mother-daughter pairs in the family, Mama and I get along the best. That's because we're both dedicated to walking the straight path. It's easy to disagree when one generation spends the afternoon gossiping on the phone and the next is shut up in her room, listening to Madonna. It's harder when you bow your heads to God together.

Close as we are, I always know when Mama's upset. "What's the matter?"

She pressed her lips together. "We can talk about it later."

"No, Mama, look at me. What's wrong? Is it—did something happen in Iraq? Palestine?"

Mama managed a little laugh, shaky and out of breath. "The things you think, Nadia. Of course not." Bassam stood up to give her his chair, and she sank into the plaid upholstery. I tried not to notice how tattered it was.

"Auntie, if you don't want to, you don't have to talk." That was Bassam, head tilted, face the picture of concern. "But it might make you feel better."

She tried to say "Nothing important," but the words wouldn't come out. Tears fell instead, coursing over her still-lovely cheeks, soaking into the gold embroidery at the neck of her *galabiya*. "Mohammad," she said. "That was Mohammad on the phone just now."

Nassir rolled off the couch and came around, reaching out an awkward arm to Mama. The second hand on the clock ticked off each of my heartbeats.

"It's all right. I mean, it could be so much worse, I shouldn't be crying, I should be thanking God for my blessings but . . . Mohammad lost his job."

"He'll find another one," Bassam said. He spoke in such a matter-of-fact tone that I was sure, almost sure, he'd been prepared for this. Lifting the edge of the couch a few inches off the floor, he dragged it forward, setting it down close enough to Mama that he could sit on the couch's edge and rest his elbows on the arm of her chair. "Mohammad is a brilliant engineer, and I'm sure it wasn't anything he did. They were probably *downsizing*." He used the English word.

Mama repeated it. "Downsizing," she said. "That's the word he used. The company had to discharge some employees, and they had to choose the foreign ones first. That's the law. He'll be home a week from Monday." She looked around our tiny apartment— two bedrooms, one salon, one very small kitchen, one bathroom, and one shower. A balcony. A couple of tiny hallways. Not even a ground-floor flat, where the overwhelmed could escape into the garden. "He and Sarah and the two girls." Dimah was two and still in diapers. Mariam, at five, was an absolute terror. The last time she stayed with us, she broke Mama's bed by jumping on it and tried to flush a frog down the toilet. It climbed out when Auntie Um Suheil was using the facilities.

"He's coming home?" Bassam frowned. He wasn't looking at Mama but addressed his question to the floor. "He couldn't extend his visa?"

Mama's shoulders shook again. "I don't know," she said. "I don't think he could. He already has the plane tickets."

We were all silent. I was trying to avoid the thought crashing around my head: what will we live on now?

"Mohammad will find a new job in no time, don't worry, Auntie."

I glared at Bassam with his cheery voice and false hopes. Why didn't he ask Nassir how easy it was to find an engineering job in Syria? He'd scoured every corner of Damascus for three years now and still ended up empty-handed.

I wanted to say "This is an absolute disaster." I wanted to throw myself on my bed and tear out my hair and run my fingernails across my cheeks. Of course, Mama had already done those things. I wanted to shock them, spitting out all the foul language I wasn't supposed to know.

"You know who's to blame, don't you?" said Fowzi. He'd been quiet so long I'd almost forgotten he was in the room. "Thanks go to Mr. Bush, driving the regional economy into the ground for the sake of his oil-guzzling buddies."

Bassam scowled. "You can't really believe that?"

Fowzi tapped his feet on the floor. "We all know what you think, Bassam—America to the rescue, riding in to save the poor damsel-in-distress Iraqis."

Bassam continued patting Mama's arm but his mouth crinkled in annoyance. "I never said occupation is good for Iraq. The Americans make plenty of mistakes, but you're wrong if you think they make them deliberately. I know Americans, I'm friends with Americans," he added, as though this made him an expert on world affairs. "My boss in the Emirates is an American. They honestly want to help." Bassam used to be as clear-eyed about American greed as any of us. Had his Filipina girlfriend changed his mind? I pressed my lips together. A few stray thoughts, and I had Bassam doing the forbidden with an imaginary girl. May God forgive me.

"This is all about oil," said Fowzi. He clenched the briefcase so tightly his knuckles turned white. "Plain and simple—the Americans saw an opportunity to come in and grant oil contracts to Bush's friends, and they took it."

"And all this arguing gets Mohammad another job—how?" Nassir began his sentence in a reasonable voice, but by the end he was almost shouting. "We're all screwed—does it really matter whose fault it is?" He vaulted Mama's outstretched legs, side-stepped Bassam, and then ducked into his room. The slam of the door echoed in the salon, louder than any comment we might have made.

# In the Name of God,
## the Sustainer,
## the Provider

An hour later, I nudged Nassir's bedroom door open with my knee. Behind me, in the salon, Bassam and Fowzi ranted on about overtime and golden goals. How useful football is, giving men something to talk about when they have nothing to say. Mama had recovered enough to start listing the necessities we'd need to make the apartment comfortable for Mohammad and his family.

I should have known. Nassir hadn't thrown himself facedown on the bed but stood behind his schoolboy desk, untangling a stretch of wire. Computer parts covered every square inch of desk except the space reserved for a monitor the size of a television screen with a long scratch down one side. Beside it stood a box-like rectangle made of metal, covered with rows of tiny holes. Nassir pressed a button on the front of the rectangle and something whirred inside but the monitor remained dark. "Hey," I said. "Is this mess the reason Mama refuses to clean your room these days?"

"You know, if Alina wanted something from Syria that she couldn't buy in her home country, I'd send it to her." He wasn't looking at me, he was staring at a tiny screwdriver he held in one hand.

"What do we have in Syria that she can't get at home? Falafel?"

He used the screwdriver to pry open the top of the metal box. Inside were a series of flat green pieces interspersed with tiny gold circles. "Lots of things. Mother of pearl boxes. Hubble-bubble pipes. I've been writing to her for a year, and in every letter I ask for a CD-R drive, and does she ever send it to me? Or even mention that she's trying to get it?"

I picked up a handful of screws smaller than my smallest fingernail. "Don't touch anything," he said.

I dropped the screws on the desk. "Doesn't Alina live in Poland? Maybe you should find a pen friend in South Korea or Japan."

"Maybe you should ride a donkey; it's better than being one."

I bit back my harsh retort, something about better a donkey than a dog. After a minute he told me, "This is it, you know. All my hopes were pinned on Mohammad finding me work in the Emirates. God, I wish I was a girl."

I must have misheard.

"You lot have such an easy life."

An easy life? Was he joking? What did he know about period pains and men leering at you in the street and having to beg Mama just to go to the corner shop alone?

Fiddling with the nearest green metal plate, Nassir said, "Do I have a job? No. Did I get one after graduation? No. They hired only girls, because no one wants to train someone who's going into the army in a few months."

"That's not true. Lots of men get jobs—"

"No, they don't." He picked up the tiniest wrench I'd ever seen and used it to separate one part of the metal plate from another. "No one got a job. We went into the army, froze our asses off, ate stale bread for two years, and all the girls got married."

I wasn't going to let him have things all his own way. "If a girl waits to get married, she'll find all the boys in her class offering for her younger sister."

Nassir's hand was steady as he slid the bottom of the plate one quarter of an inch. "She's got a job, a husband, probably a baby by now, a house—no girl with a degree would marry a man who lives with his parents—and two incomes. We're out of the living hell that's the army and what's left for us? Waiting tables?"

I picked up a thin screwdriver that ended in a metal square. "Nassir, you'll find a job and get married—"

"Could you leave my tools alone, please? And no, I won't. Only three guys from my class have jobs, and one of those is Mahmoud, whose father owns United Arab Engineering. The other two are Alawis." Alawis. It's not only Nassir who thinks they get the best of everything just because they belong to the same Shia sect as the president. "To think about marriage you need to have first, a house, and then money for furniture, and money for her wedding clothes and jewelry. And once you have all that, you need still more money for the bride gift."

"Nassir, Nassir," I said, when he finally took a breath. "You know that men and women each have rights and responsibilities in Islam, and they—"

"Men have all the responsibilities and women have all the rights, Nadia." He pushed the metal plate a little harder. "Even after marriage. Take the typical young family. Husband, wife, and two kids. Husband works, wife works. Husband pays rent, buys all the clothes, all the food, pays all the transportation. Wife works, buys bracelets to line her arms."

Not every Syrian family lives like that. I pictured myself leaning out of the window of a villa, watching as my two young sons splash in the sea. Tall and lean, with wide eyes and wild hair, they look like Fowzi. "Don't go out far, boys, you know your mother worries." But my husband's only teasing, he rests his chin on the top of my head and laughs . . . .

"That's not every family, Nassir. Fine, you're angry, but you have to be fair, too."

"Esam and Fatima."

"That's *one* couple, Nassir."

"Aamar and Feyrouz. Mustapha and Shehanaz."

So what if most women don't contribute to the family income? Nassir was missing one important point. If there's a divorce, all that stuff, the house and the furniture and the car and even the kids, the husband collects it all. The wife needs her bracelets because if things don't work out, that gold is all she's got.

The bottom plate finally slid out, and Nassir tilted it onto the desk without touching it. "What gets me," he said, "is those Western feminists. You see them on CNN or Egyptian talk shows, spouting all their nonsense about 'Arab women are so oppressed.' When I hear that, the first thing I think? Lady, you never met an Arab woman."

I watched as he surveyed the inside of the box again. "You have all kinds of rights and privileges you take for granted, Nassir. You come home at eleven thirty at night, and no one notices. If I'm ten minutes late after school, I get the third degree."

He snapped the box closed. "If that's all I had to put up with, in exchange for marrying my way into a life of ease, I'd become a woman in a second."

"They have those operations in America, you know. People there change gender all the time."

Nassir grimaced. "Like they'd give me a visa for that." Leaning forward he pushed the button again. *Whir, purr* inside, a long minute of waiting, and then a flash across the screen. "You fixed it!" I said. Maybe I should have kept the surprise out of my voice, but Nassir didn't seem to mind. *Microsoft Windows 98*, I read, followed by a little multicolored flag that waved on the screen.

I moved to the door, calling Mama and Fowzi and Bassam to come and see his success, letting the computer have the last word.

# In the Name of God,
## the Fashioner

The rest of the week passed in a daze of turning out blankets and donating clothes and shifting rooms, so that Mohammad's family could have some small measure of privacy. Mama brought out her silver candlesticks, the ones my grandmother gave her when Mohammad was born, and put them on the side table in Nasser's old bedroom. "They're a little plain," she said, moving them an inch closer to the bed. "But Sarah's so modern, maybe she'll like plain."

Sarah likes plain about as much as your average princess.

The doorbell rang before I could say anything, though. Gossip in Damascus travels with the pollen—in and out of windows, unseen but never unfelt. The very day after Mohammad called Mama, relatives showed up with kisses and sympathy, leaving small gifts we didn't find until after they'd left. A canister of tea, a sack of oranges, a roll of fifty-pound notes. Mama cried when she found each one.

I didn't cry at all, not even on Thursday afternoon, when Mama sent me to the corner vegetable stand and I saw the cardboard signs sticking out of the piles of vegetables, the crossed-out prices raised at least five lira. My hundred-lira note wouldn't buy both onions and tomatoes. That meant either a sauce that tasted like dust pudding, or no sauce at all.

"I'll give you fifty lira a kilo for those tomatoes, and it's still highway robbery," said Auntie Um Suheil, bustling up beside me. "Nadia, it's so good to see you here. How's your mama?"

"Fine."

She eyed down the half-grown boy behind the folding table

until he dropped the kilo weight on one side of the scale and filled the other with his choicest tomatoes. "Did you want some too, Nadia?"

He scowled at me, but I ignored him. "A kilo and a half," I said. "Onions, too."

I got it all for ninety lira and the pleasure of Auntie Um Suheil's company. She leaned heavily on my arm as we headed toward the crosswalk. "I'm so glad we have this chance for a private talk," she told me. Unaccustomed to much walking, she panted a little. "Have you spoken to her—your cousin, the plump one, Yasmine? She's been seen you know."

"What are you talking about?"

"I hear the boy is from Mezzah," she went on. "Very wealthy. She's making the same mistake as so many girls though—cheap won't catch you a flashy guy. You're so proper and serious, Nadia, you must have some influence over her."

"I don't know what you're talking about," I said again. Yasmine might know the latest pop songs better than her prayers, but she hadn't lost all sight of the straight path. She knew better than to spend time with a strange boy. *Come not nigh to adultery: it is an indecent deed and an evil way.*

"You should warn her to be more careful, Nadia—that brother of hers is a bit of a zealot."

Fowzi? A zealot? Take your religion seriously and get called a fundie by nasty old gossips with nothing better to do. We reached the corner and I shook her off, heading to the beggar in his familiar place below the traffic light.

Only when I drew near did I realize my friend with the crumpled leg was missing. A bent old man sat in his place, rocking back and forth, a pile of pink and green pamphlets at his feet. Bending over, I dropped my last ten-pound note into his grizzled palm. The old beggar mumbled his thanks, rifling through his pamphlets.

I had almost turned away when he looked up. He wasn't as old as I'd thought. Not old at all, actually. His face was lined with grime, not wrinkles, and the dirty hand he held out was steady. Dark brown eyes met mine, unashamed. Just for a moment, then he lowered his gaze.

Auntie Um Suheil bustled up, a handful of coins clinking in her palm. She dropped them onto the green cloth spread out at his feet. "Do you have to walk so fast, Nadia?" she complained. "Have a little mercy for an old woman, please."

"Here, kind madam," said the beggar, holding out a leaflet. "A few verses from the Qur'an, to carry the words of God close to your heart."

A coincidence? Was it my imagination that spotted the drunken lurcher everywhere? The young man I'd seen that night, the gawker in Mukhayim Yarmuk, this beggar—they all had the same build, the same way of holding their head to one side, the same casual strength. A grace you didn't often see on a beggar. Would a street income support an alcohol habit, or the spotless clothes worn by the youth in Yarmuk?

"Please, kind lady," he said. "I have nothing else to give."

Arms full of bags, Auntie Um Suheil shook her head. "No hands, no hands," she said. "Can't you see?" She snorted a little and looked away.

The casual grace was gone, flown with my imagination. He was ragged, battered by life, and poor. Not a young man to careen from drink or gape at girls. He moved his hand slightly, now offering the scraps of paper to me. His gaze was focused on the ground. I didn't think he was the kind of young man who hissed or took liberties, just waiting for the opportunity to pinch me, to whisper, *Oh pretty, oh beautiful, come here to me.* He held the papers by their very edge, leaving me room to pluck them without touching his hand.

I took them. The light changed and Auntie Um Suheil found a hand to clutch my arm, pulling me off the curb. She prattled on about her nieces, domestic divas who embroidered for cash. I shifted the bag of tomatoes and onions to the crook of my elbow and looked down at the leaflet in my hand. Ornate Arabic, as I'd expected, with all the vowels marked. The beginning of that comforting Qur'an verse, *God is closer to the heart of the believer than the jugular vein.* And then . . . .

We reached the sidewalk on the other side of the street, and I twisted my head around for one last look. The beggar sat up, not even pretending not to be interested. He was staring straight across the empty street, staring at me. His brown eyes were still respectful, but there was something else there, too. Challenge. It's an amazing thing, perspective. He didn't look grimy to me anymore, or dirty or unkempt. He looked like a soldier.

I rubbed my lips together and looked down at the paper again.

*Dear Sister, are you one of those whose heart belongs to God?*

*Please let a respectful brother invite you to join our worship.*

That was all. Almost all. Underneath, someone had snipped a piece of green paper into a thin rectangle. Dull green paper, universally recognized. *In God We Trust,* it said. In English.

# In the Name of God, the Majestic

> *Hold fast, all together, by the rope which God stretches out for you, and be not divided among yourselves; and remember with gratitude God's favor on you; for you were enemies and He joined your hearts in love, so that by His Grace, you became brothers; and you were on the brink of the pit of fire, and He saved you from it.*

Alone on the balcony with His book, I searched for verses about the responsibility of the Believers to band together for the sake of the Muslim Nation. Whenever I found one, I ran my finger beneath each word, sounding out the elegant classical Arabic syllable by syllable. Between verses, I couldn't help thinking about the beggar, and that no one would know better than Fowzi how to answer an invitation to rebellion.

Then I was no longer alone. "I'm so pleased to see you reading Qur'an, Nadia," said Mama, a smile in her voice, a cousin at her heels. "There's no better way to spend a Friday morning."

"What verse are you reading?" asked Samira, pulling up a plastic chair and plunking down next to me. A little awkward at first, I recited the verse out loud; as I gained confidence, Samira joined in. God's rhythm and cadence, sung on Samira's lips, in my voice, enchanted the heart more than any human song. I drowned in the mystery and depth of His million-meaning words. Even the silence that filled the balcony as our words faded away paid homage to God's glory.

Samira plucked a leaf off the overhanging tree and twirled it between her fingers. "It's amazing how harmonious God's creation is," she said. "And how we humans ruin it."

"Is that what you think the verse means?" asked Mama.

Samira spun her leaf so hard the stem broke. "I think so. We need to reach out to our enemies, see that we all share the world together. How terrible and sad that more Muslims don't read Qur'an and see its peace for themselves."

A warm wind rustled the pages of the Holy Book, the ends of my scarf, the petals of the white flowers blooming in Mama's cracked pot.

I meant to say nothing, but I'm not very good at that. "This verse isn't talking about reaching out to enemies—it's talking about banding together against them."

Samira snorted. Mama's lips formed a thin line. "That's not what the text says," Mama told me. "You can't read your own meanings into the Word of God; that's innovation."

Innovation. Elevating your own ideas beside God's creation. Few words put more fear into the heart of a Believer. "I'm not innovating, Mama," I said. I thought of Fowzi, clever enough to outwit self-righteous progressives like Bassam, and brave enough that he didn't care who heard him. I might not be shouting slogans in the street, but at least I could stand up to Mama. "If you believe that we're supposed to make nice with the Unbelievers, you're not paying attention to the news."

"The Prophet—may peace be upon him—made peace with the Unbelievers, in case you've forgotten," said Samira. She tilted her chair so far back it balanced against the balcony railing. "He forgave all the Meccans who'd fought against him, welcomed them into the community, and even gave some of them important positions."

"Only after they accepted Islam," I pointed out. "I guess I must have missed those CNN photos of George Bush bowing to Mecca."

"Girls!" Mama clapped her hands together. "That's enough. Friday is a day of prayer and devotion, not a time to snipe at each other." I bowed my head, more than a little embarrassed to be caught acting like a primary-school girl. Samira must have done the same, because Mama said, "That's better."

When I looked up, Samira had straightened her chair and sat with her legs curled up under her. She said, "Muslims need to stop worrying about what the Unbelievers are doing and concentrate on ourselves."

I swung my legs back and forth under my chair. "I don't care what the infidels do in their own corrupt countries. They can prance naked in the street, drink alcohol till they forget their own names, leave all their property to their cats. God will deal with that. My problem with the infidels is that they interfere with us."

I gave them a chance, but neither Mama nor Samira spoke up. "That's why bin Laden bombed the towers," I continued. "Because he wanted America to stop supporting our enemies. Israel and the repressive regimes that imprison pious men." Samira's eyes opened wide, and Mama's hands began tapping the edge of the Qur'an. "Like Egypt."

"So, now you think bombing three thousand innocent people was a blow for Islamic rights?" Samira's eyes flashed.

"If it even was bin Laden." I didn't care if I contradicted myself. "Thousands of Jews worked in the towers and not one of them showed up for work that day. Someone called them all and told them to stay home. There are more Jews in New York City than in Tel Aviv and not one was killed. Do you think bin Laden arranged that?"

Samira shook her head, scorn oozing out with every swoosh of her dark hair. "That's only a rumor, Nadia—there were Jewish people in the towers when the planes hit. Not even Israel would risk the wrath of mighty Uncle Sam that way."

"I think Bush did it himself," I said. I wrapped one hand around the top rail. "It gave him the excuse he needed to go into Iraq."

For the third time, Mama tried to put an end to the debate. "We'll never know what happened that day in September, will we?" she said. "It was a tragedy; all we can do is hope that God will show mercy to the families of those who died."

"Tens of thousands of Iraqis are dead, Baghdad's a pile of

smoking rubble, and we're still talking about three thousand people who died when a building collapsed?" Somehow my own words only made me angrier. "Why are their lives always worth more than ours?" I felt so helpless. What could I do, a lone *hijabi* girl? No armor to stop their tanks, no platform to challenge their lies.

I kicked at the railing, but my foot slipped and slammed into Mama's cracked flowerpot. It hurtled through the air and crashed into the garden below. Mama's mouth rounded into small O. She looked horrified.

Downstairs, the sliding glass door screeched open and members of Auntie Um Suheil's family rushed to be first at the scene of the flowerpot invasion. Mama and Samira bent over the rail, absorbed in the scene below. I couldn't stand it anymore. I could hardly sign on to some anonymous beggar's underground army— proper young ladies didn't do that sort of thing, ditto girls who wanted to go to medical school. But I couldn't do nothing anymore either.

I left. Just like that, I backed away from the balcony, passed through my bedroom, the salon, the hallway, and kept right on going. At the front door, I paused. A murmur of voices fluttered in from the balcony. Mama and Samira offering explanations to those below? The murmur sounded more rhythmic than that—almost as though Mama were reciting Qur'an. The thought comforted me. I'd embarrassed her, but she wasn't about to betray me to Auntie Um Suheil.

I pushed open the door. Not the door to the kitchen, but the door to outside. As I passed out of the apartment, Mama raised her voice. *"In the Name of God, the All Compassionate, the All Merciful."* I tripped down the steps, clunked past Auntie Um Suheil's door, headed into the garden. I had no idea where I was going, but it had to be better than here.

## In the Name of God,
## the All Knowing

"Nadia!" My cousin's voice floated through the air.
Still several feet from the corner of the garden, I squelched my impulse to ignore Samira and turned around. Not Samira but her sister stood there, and behind her, Fowzi. I smelled the aroma coming from the packages in his arms before I saw them: mouthwatering roast chicken.

Trapped or saved? I waited at the edge of the path until they caught up. "Where are you going?" asked Yasmine. She rearranged the bottom of her T-shirt, which revealed a shocking glimpse of belly skin when she moved. As usual, just that much more brazen than her sister. "Where's Samira?"

"*Salaam aleikum,* Cousin," said Fowzi. "We came to kidnap you—and Samira and Nassir—for a picnic at Tishreen Park. What do you say?"

What could I say? "*Aleikum salaam.* Samira's upstairs, on the balcony with Mama."

"I'll go," said Yasmine. Her heels clicked on the path, then clattered up the stairs.

Fowzi and I were alone in the garden. In the distance, cars honked as they raced each other down the highway; overhead a plane whirred its way to Europe or the Gulf. Up close, the chicken scent seeping from the packages mingled with the faint odor of spicy soap and a fragrant trace of jasmine. Not for the first time, the future distracted me. *Fowzi will make some woman a wonderful husband.* I saw him hunched over the kitchen sink, arms submerged up to the elbows in suds, while I sat at the table, head buried in my medical books. Or maybe reading out loud from an inspiring text. Fowzi would have part of the book memorized and he'd chime in with his opinion now and again. A soft breeze would blow in, and somewhere in the background, a baby cooed . . . .

"Cousin?" Fowzi's voice brought me back to the breezeless, babyless present. "It's like you're a million miles away."

I twirled the end of my scarf. "Just thinking about how important it is to spend time with the right people. People who care about their religion, who can help me stay on the straight path." In Islam, truth is mandatory, details optional.

"You think about that too?"

Alone with Fowzi. Something clicked. For the first time in days I had a chance to ask him about the blue book, the identity card. I could get his opinion on the beggar's note too, although I felt strangely reluctant to talk about that. It seemed private, personal, almost the way I felt about my prayers. I'd have to be more subtle than the time I cornered him at the party, less clumsy than the way I'd just challenged Samira.

Trying hard to word my question just right, I missed the first half of Fowzi's sentence. ". . . but you're so young."

"What?"

A bee, buzzing from flower to flower, skimmed the edge of my skirt. I stood absolutely still.

"I've been meaning to talk to you about something, Nadia, but every time I have the opportunity, I, well, I back away. I worry that your mother will blame me for putting ideas into your head, wonder how committed you are to a career in medicine . . . ."

What? This wasn't how I'd pictured my first marriage proposal. Dusty garden, droning bees, brutal sun. A balcony lit by the stars—that's more like it—soft classical music rising to a crescendo, an evening breeze rippling around my ankles. Me in a white dress with a snow-white scarf, Fowzi in—maybe not a suit and tie, but at least his hands wouldn't be sticky with chicken grease! And he'd have a bouquet of deep red flowers . . . .

Another scene interrupted my thoughts. Fowzi still at the

sudsy sink, I at the kitchen table, copying notes out of a physiology book. Only this time, in the background, I hear a baby wailing. A little boy whines, "Give it to me, it's mine!" Instead of reciting inspirational quotes, Fowzi says, "It's your turn to deal with them, I've been at work all day." I answer, petulant, irritated, not my real voice at all, "If I don't get this memorized by tomorrow, I'll fail the course."

Fowzi was staring over my head, adjusting the hot packages in his arms. It wasn't that I didn't love him—was it?—but it was too soon. Surely we had years for this?

"What's taking Yasmine and Samira so long?" I was embarrassed to change the subject, but more embarrassed not to. "I'll go and see, shall I?"

He didn't look at me as I backed away. Was he thinking *I knew it, too young* or *I'll wait for her to grow up*? Did I want to know?

I made my way up the stairs, face flushed, hands shaking. The front door was ajar. From our tiny kitchen, I heard voices caught up in conversation. "Mumble, mumble, mumble"—a man. Then a woman, her voice light and high. A young woman. Not Mama.

*A man and a woman alone together, the devil is with them.* I should have walked right in; giving someone space for forbidden activities is hardly Islamic, or even kind. Instead, I slipped out of my shoes and slid inside the door, making myself tiny against the space of wall before the kitchen.

"He's forgotten already," said Nassir. "Trust me on this."

Long sigh, low voice. "I can't do that." Yasmine. "Can't you talk to him? Find out what went wrong, why he doesn't want to . . . I know he doesn't love me, right now. But you could tell him, he'll never find another girl who loves him as much as I do."

So Auntie Um Suheil had been right. A sick feeling started in my stomach, climbed up into my chest and settled there. I'd known Yasmine liked the glamour-girl life, but I never thought she'd take it to this extreme.

"I wish I'd never introduced you."

"Meeting Mahmoud is the only important thing that's ever happened to me."

Mahmoud? She couldn't mean Mahmoud Sharki. Yasmine with her short skirts and her bangle bracelets and her perfectly coiffed hair, in love with short, skinny, never-prays Mahmoud? Mama had counseled Nassir against his company in a roundabout way. I'd been much more blunt. "God will judge you by the company you keep, on the Day of Reckoning," I told him. "And since Mahmoud is the next thing to an Unbeliever, you don't want to be standing near him."

"Things aren't going to work out the way you want them to, Yasmine. Mahmoud's not even thinking about marriage."

Something clinked. Yasmine, fiddling with her bracelets? "I don't want him to marry me, I just want him to love me." Her voice cracked with desperation.

*In the name of God*, I mouthed in my hidden corner, thanking Him for protecting me from the humiliation of illicit relations. What had gone wrong for Yasmine? Weak will, the devil at her elbow? Lax parenting and a poverty that made even the smallest luxury hard to come by? Or just too many Western films steeped in boyfriends and love before marriage?

"I'd be happy if we lived together in a shack with no proper bathroom and had bread and hummus every meal."

"You wouldn't. Mahmoud is not a nice person." Nassir sighed. "I know you think he is because he's charming, and he flatters you, but he's not nice at all. He's selfish, and he'll say anything to get what he wants."

I heard the shift of a chair as someone pushed back from the table. "Then why are you friends with him?"

I had already slid my feet back into my shoes, but I waited because I'd always wanted to know the answer to this. "We went to school together, we've been friends for twenty years. There's something to being loyal to a person, no matter what they've done." There was a pause. "And Mahmoud's father owns United Arab Engineering. They've got a contract for a whole set of bridges in the north. They're going to need engineers and he's promised to talk about me. There's no other way to get a job in this country," he added. Was he trying to convince Yasmine or himself? "I've tried everything else—cold-calling companies, job fairs, expensive afternoons at Internet cafes. No one's even looked at my resume on that Syrian engineers' Web site. It all comes down to who you know."

I stepped back into the hall and eased shut the door in front of me. One, two, three—a deep breath and as loud a knock as I could manage.

# In the Name of God, the Guardian of Faith

The day, bright and sunny, was welcoming to picnickers, and we wandered among dozens of dining families before we found a spot to spread our plastic tablecloth. By the time we set out our feast—chicken, garlic mayonnaise, fresh bread, and two former Pepsi bottles reinvented as water jars—I had my riotous emotions mostly in check. Except that I'd started thinking in headlines. *Misguided Yasmine Meets Mahmoud: Auntie Um Suheil Right for Once.* Or this one: *Nadia Nixes Nuptials: Will She Regret It Forever?* Fine. I sounded more like a soap opera than a newspaper. That didn't stop the lines from playing themselves over and over inside my head.

I ate little and spoke less. No one seemed to notice. Not Samira and Yasmine, dissecting a recent wedding; not Nassir, off on one of his endless offside rants. Certainly not Fowzi, chiming in on one conversation or the other between bites of chicken. I couldn't even glance at him. Except that I must have, because I caught him looking far more cheerful than a rejected suitor had any right to. And I noticed the minute he stiffened and sat up straight. "Look," he said, pointing. "It's Bassam."

I stiffened, too. Yasmine, showing no such compunction, dabbed her mayonnaise-spotted mouth with the edge of the tablecloth, then turned around and waved. Bassam and his companion, a thin, pale man in faded blue jeans and an expensive foreign shirt, moved in our direction.

*"Salaam aleikum,"* said Bassam, much too soon for my taste. He leaned over and shook hands with us one by one before introducing his skinny companion. "An old friend of mine, Jalil, from

engineering school. Jalil, the most important members of my family, from left to right: Samira, Yasmine, Nadia, Nassir, Fowzi." Jalil didn't reach out to shake anybody's hand, nor did he put his hand over his heart to indicate he followed the Prophet's example and never shook hands with women. Instead he gave an awkward little wave. Bassam explained, after a fashion, "Jalil's over on a visit from the States."

"Really?" Yasmine's big eyes widened. "Do you live in New York? Or Hollywood?"

It was about time one of us remembered our manners. No surprise, it was Fowzi who said, "Please. Sit down. Join us for lunch, there's plenty for everyone."

Bassam began to protest but Jalil took a seat on the tablecloth without further urging and made himself a sandwich, tearing off strips of chicken, slathering it with mayonnaise, and sticking it inside the warm bread.

"Please," Samira said. "Help yourself."

Bassam eased into a kneeling position between Yasmine and me and waved away Samira's offer of a sandwich.

"It's been a long time since I've had hot bread like this," said Jalil. "I've been in the States for seven years, studying."

Again I keyed into Fowzi's slight movement, raising his head and staring at Jalil before he spoke. Then he asked only, "What do you study?"

"Civil engineering. I finished four years ago, but the visa process in America is so complicated that I couldn't leave. Now I have my green card, I can come and go as I please, and the first place I came was home."

"Did they arrest you?" The words were out of my mouth before I could stop them. Better to start an argument than sit sulking in the corner. "I heard they arrested all Muslim men in America after September eleventh."

Jalil made a funny sound, a cross between a laugh and a snort. His mouth still full of bread, he waited till he swallowed before answering. "Why does everyone keep asking me that? No, they didn't arrest all Muslim men." He shrugged. "There are eight million Muslims in America, you know. They could hardly arrest us all. Even if they could—Muslims have the freedom to come and go as we please, like everyone else. Even if they had a place to lock us up, they wouldn't bother."

"Eight million," said Samira. "I didn't know that. Some Muslim countries don't have that many Muslims."

"Don't the American secret police spy on the mosques?" I asked. "That's what I heard."

Jalil tore off another piece of bread. "Everyone' s so ready to believe the worst of America," he said, not bothering to look around or lower his voice. "As though the mosques here are so secret police–free."

Samira coughed. I couldn't help it, I scanned the nearby gardens. Bassam, perhaps the most prepared to change the subject, intervened. "America is a large country, so there are probably different experiences, depending where you live. For example, New York is full of crime, but then you see TV shows, like *Bold and Beautiful*, and these people lead rich and happy lives."

Yasmine tossed her thick hair over her shoulders, scenting the breeze with the smell of shampoo and hairspray. "Did you see last week's episode?" she began. "The one where Brooke—"

"I don't watch *Bold and Beautiful*," I said. I wiped my fingers on one of the paper napkins Fowzi had brought. "Anyway, I don't think they lead happy lives, always being with each other's husbands."

Bassam looked at me. "I don't like the show either," he said. "The same thing happens over and over."

Jalil didn't seem interested in discussing soap operas. "American Muslims have the same vote as everyone else. The ballot box, the great equalizer." More chicken, more mayo, more bread. "Damn, this is good," he added. "I'll have to come home more often."

Fowzi reached across his sister for the Pepsi bottle of water. "So you think democracy is the great solution?" he asked.

Jalil rubbed his lips together. "I didn't say that."

"And when the Americans vote to herd all Muslims into concentration camps, what will you say then?" Jalil didn't say anything, maybe because his mouth was too stuffed with chicken. Fowzi went on, "Democracy is a hoax. Only when the word of God is the foundation of government can you protect everyone's rights."

"Are you saying," asked Bassam, "that all states should be Islamic? In other words, you think we should have an Islamic government in Syria?"

With that sentence, the conversation, teetering on the edge of dangerous, jumped to deadly. *Don't answer, Fowzi.* I looked around for help. The girls plucked strands of grass from the ground, Nassir stared at his shoes. "Every Muslim has the right to live according to Islamic law," said Fowzi, as though he didn't care who heard him, as though the secret police wore earplugs. "And I don't think a democratic system can ever guarantee that."

Had Fowzi lost his mind? A call for Islamic law is the most dangerous statement a Syrian can make.

"If Muslims in America have it so good," said Samira, riding to the rescue at last, "then why aren't they helping the rest of us? I read an article in *al Ahram* that interviewed Muslims living in America, and they couldn't fly in planes anymore, so they had to drive all the way across the country to their new jobs."

"Yes," I said. "And what about right after September eleventh? I heard fourteen hundred Muslims were attacked in retaliation. I heard that Muslim girls in America are afraid to wear their veils."

Jalil finished the rest of his second sandwich and wiped his fingers before saying, "What do you think—I paddled a canoe ten thousand kilometers?"

"You what?"

"Do you think I came by boat? Muslims can still fly. Just they maybe question you a little more. And nobody attacked *me* after

9/11." Jalil took out a pack of cigarettes and tapped one into the palm of his hand. "Americans are so uptight about where you smoke. You can't even take out a cigarette in a restaurant, and I should know, I've tried."

None of us looked at him. We all knew that cigarettes originated in America, and we'd all seen plenty of tourists, even women tourists, smoking one after another, so what was he talking about? "Look, I'm not saying America is perfect. There are lots of Americans who are racist against Muslims—who call 'murderer' or 'terrorist' after you in the street, who won't sit next to you in class in case you have a bomb. This girl I know who converted, her own brother tore the scarf off her head. But let me tell you, in terms of being able to say what you want, even about religion—America is much better than here."

Too bad he didn't remember that before he made comments the secret police would haul him off to Tadmor Prison for. Him and us, just for listening. Then Yasmine asked, "Have you seen the latest Jackie Chan film?" Of course, being Yasmine, maybe she wasn't avoiding a dangerous subject but really wanted to know.

Jalil started to answer her, but Fowzi wasn't content to let the moment pass. "Don't you think," he said to Jalil, "that, as a Muslim, your first responsibility is to the Muslim community? How can you be responsible to the Muslims when you live in a state that's attacking them?"

"I don't think there's any conflict between being a U.S. resident and being a Muslim." Jalil leaned back, letting a thin trickle of smoke mar the perfect afternoon. Then he added, "Besides, the war in Iraq is complicated. I don't agree with everything the U.S. has done there, but getting rid of Saddam Hussein—no one can deny that was a favor to the Iraqis."

"A favor to the Iraqis?" Fowzi clenched his hands. "Filling their country with foreign soldiers and bombs blasting on every corner?"

"Don't you think the insurgents are responsible for their own actions?" asked Jalil, still calm, still smoking. "As we all are, according to the Qur'an."

"And rightly so," said Fowzi. He had regained control of his voice, if not his comments. "Every Muslim should rise up against oppression, whatever form it takes—occupying power, repressive regime, whoever. It's our responsibility to band together with whatever weapons we have—bombs if we can make them, words if we can say them, our bodies if that's all we have left."

Once again, Fowzi's words took my breath away. They transformed him from a skinny, diffident youth into a warrior. I stared down at my *manteau*-covered thighs. How could I want to shake him for his lack of caution and hug him for his bravery at the exact same moment?

Jalil flicked the ash of his cigarette onto the ground. Stinky, smelly cancer sticks—one more example of America peddling death around the world. "Funny," he said. "In the U.S., I'm always arguing against the war—I never would have thought I'd get home and find myself arguing for it."

Later, after Bassam and Jalil headed off for the duty-free shops, the rest of us took a taxi to our apartment. I hung back as Fowzi argued with Nassir over who would pay the driver. We headed to the stairs en masse, and I turned to him, my question ready—*What on earth were you thinking?*—but he got in first. "Nadia, could you make my apologies to your mother? I have to meet a friend in Salheya; he's got legal troubles and I promised him I'd try to help him sort them out. I'm late already, so . . . I'll have to take a rain check on the coffee."

"I really need to talk to you." We reached the bottom of the stairs. Nassir, halfway home, paused on the landing. "You can't just go on like that in public, Fowzi, and in front of people you don't know."

"I didn't say anything dangerous."

"Fowzi! You said . . ." I couldn't repeat it. Nassir disappeared into the shadows. "I just don't understand you anymore."

Fowzi pressed his hands together. The lobby, dim in the fading afternoon light, made it impossible for me to read the expression on his face. "There's nothing to understand, Cousin. Don't you think I know what I'm doing?"

No. I didn't. So many ways I could tell him that, none that I could actually force past my lips.

"You think this guy's a spy for the CIA?"

Any minute now, Auntie Um Suheil would come out of her apartment and catch me alone in the almost-dark with a boy. By tomorrow noon, it'll be all over town that I'm as flighty as my cousin—*puts up a respectable front, that Nadia, but no better than she should be and not half as good as we thought*. I edged toward the stairs. "You know very well it's not the CIA I'm worried about."

"Nadia, don't worry. I know what I'm doing." He moved toward the stone path. In the illumination of Auntie Um Suheil's front lamp, he looked thinner, but not gaunt. High-cheekboned and noble, maybe. "My *salaams* to your mama."

*Follow him.* The solution to all my mysteries might be at the end of his journey tonight. A dark, lonely alley somewhere; a clandestine meeting of men in hoods and gloves; the sickening sound of knives slicing flesh as they prepared to sign their names in blood. Fowzi stopped at the corner of the garden path and waved to me. By the time I raised my hand in return, he'd gone.

*Follow him.* I thought it like there would be no consequences. Explaining to Mama why I was three hours late would be the least of my problems. Negotiating buses, warding off strange men, avoiding pickpockets—I couldn't do any of that. Not get lost and not get caught. I could only imagine Fowzi's face if he spotted me peering through the window of the falafel shop where he and his friend bent their heads over a three-inch pile of legal documents.

For the second time that day, I headed up the stairs.

## In the Name of God, the Distressor

Samira rang me up Sunday after school. "Come and help us make *kibba*," she said. *Kibba*, the ground lamb baked in a meat and wheat germ shell that Syrians make so much better than the Lebanese do. My mouth started to water. "Bassam brought us the lamb," Samira continued. "He said no one makes *kibba* like Mama, and he wants to make sure he has some before he goes back to the Emirates. And you don't have to worry," she added, before I had time to worry, "he's not here to bother you—he left already."

"Bother me?" What was Samira thinking? "I get along fine with Bassam."

"I saw you in the park the other day. Bassam kept inching in your direction, and every time he did, you inched away." As usual, Samira's interpretation of recent history differed 180 degrees from mine. All I remembered about Bassam in the park was that he'd been surprisingly quiet. Unusual, for him.

I found Auntie and my cousins in the kitchen when I arrived an hour later. Fowzi opened the door, a book in his hand, his forefinger stuck inside to mark his place. The book was gray, not blue, but I sneaked a quick glance at the title anyway—just a Qur'an commentary, nothing illegal or forbidden. I was relieved, and somehow disappointed at the same time. Too full of feeling to say anything but *salaams*, I left him to his book and joined the women in the kitchen.

Samira stood at the counter, grinding meat. Yasmine chopped parsley at their long kitchen table while, next to her, Auntie mixed cumin into the already ground lamb. I slipped out of my *manteau* and rolled up my sleeves. "Here's another pair of hands—where

PAULA JOLIN

do you need them?" Maybe they had underestimated their own enterprise and didn't need me after all, maybe Auntie would send me to sit in the salon next to Fowzi, to listen as he read out loud from the Qur'an commentary.

"Come help me chop," said Yasmine.

"Give me a break from the grinder," said Samira.

"Yasmine, close the door so Nadia can take off her scarf," said Auntie. "And Nadia, sit at the end of the table, please, and start forming patties with this meat."

We rearranged ourselves. Yasmine didn't shut the door quite tight; a thin sliver of salon showed through at the edge, and I could see Fowzi at the end of the couch with his book. Knowing Fowzi's respectful ways, I pulled the scarf off my head anyway. Auntie passed me the heavy ceramic bowl containing the meat mixture and got up to supervise Samira at the grinder.

"I still think you're being unfair," whined Yasmine. "*Bride and Prejudice* is a perfectly respectable movie."

"I never said it wasn't," said Auntie. "If you want to go with your brother, I have no problem with that. But two girls, un-escorted, alone in a theater—anything could happen."

"Nothing's going to happen," said Yasmine. Her knife slammed down on the chopping board once, twice, three times. "Fowzi doesn't get off work in time for the showing at the cinema in Salheya—and Leila's mother wouldn't like it if he came with us anyway."

Leila? That must be the second girl. Then— "You don't want to go?" I asked Samira.

She lifted her hands off the grinder and shook them in the air. "Too much physics homework."

Auntie moved across the kitchen to the sink and washed her hands. "Nothing's going to happen," she told Yasmine, "because you're not going." I wanted to applaud Auntie's stand, but my hands were covered with sticky meat. Besides, my cousins would think I was a prude.

A sharp knock reverberated against the front door. "I'll get it, Fowzi," said Auntie, giving her hands a quick dry on a kitchen towel and grabbing my scarf off the back of the chair. I moved to one side as Auntie slipped through the kitchen doorway, but when the door fell back to its former sliver, I relaxed.

"Who could that be?" asked Samira.

Her sister didn't care. "I can't believe you're not supporting me on *Bride and Prejudice*," she said. "You know how much I want to go."

Samira shrugged. "Go with Fowzi next Friday."

We couldn't see the front door from where we sat, but we heard it swing wide as Auntie opened it. A guttural voice snapped out, "Fowzi Najjar?" No *salaams*, no introductions, nothing. Yasmine slid the elastic off a new bunch of parsley, but Samira sat listening, head cocked, as carefully as me.

"I'm Fowzi Najjar," said Fowzi. Through the sliver of doorway, I could see Fowzi start to stand up. I could see, too, two soldiers cross the other room in their green camouflage uniforms, black boots soiling Auntie's newly washed floorboards, machine guns hanging at their sides like extra limbs. What could they want with Fowzi? He looked so slim beside their hulking forms.

My heart beat faster. I got to my feet before the first soldier struck Fowzi on the head with the knuckle side of his fist. "Nooooo!" someone cried out, Auntie maybe or Fowzi himself or even me. I scraped back my chair and ran through the door, careless of my scarf, my *manteau*, my sticky fingers. "You can't hurt him, he hasn't done anything!" My words, not my voice—high pitched, squeaky, breathless with emotion.

The second soldier was already punching Fowzi in the chest, and my cousin let out a little moan. He didn't even put up his hands to protect himself. I tried to do that, tried to slip between the aggressor and his victim, but the first soldier plucked me off, held me with one arm like a child. I escaped as the second soldier moved from Fowzi's stomach to his head. "Noooo!" I pushed myself back in front of Fowzi. In a fit of impatience, the first soldier pulled me away and gave me a strong shove, slamming me against the wall. My back cracked in sharp, searing pain, and my teeth clenched, making it impossible to speak. I slumped to the floor.

Samira remained in control. "You have no right to force your way in here," she said. Her voice shook, but she used it anyway. "Where's your warrant? Where's your judge's order?" Words she'd learned from her late-night foreign TV shows. But we hadn't gone foreign, we were here, in Syria, and the soldiers dragged Fowzi through the salon without bothering to answer her. "Terrorist dog," one of them said as they reached the door. He wore a green string around his wrist, symbol of the Alawis, who rule the country, and he held it up in a mock salute.

Fowzi's battered face hung over the soldier's shoulder for the briefest moment, swollen eyes closed, red and angry bruises rising up along his hairline. A trickle of blood oozed out of the corner of his mouth. Then they were out into the hall, Fowzi half towed, half carried between the two men. The door slammed behind them. In the next few moments, the silence broken only by Auntie's muffled sobs, I tried to take it all in. Fowzi had been seized by the authorities—taken where? Why? Why was easy to answer though. His bold, brave words seemed foolhardy now, not a weapon but a joke, impotent against machine guns and pummeling fists. *I had warned him.*

My anger turned inward. Warned him, yes, but how hard? I had been impressed by his willingness to take on the government, had yearned to be more like him. Even today, I had wanted to find him reading a seditious book. Worst of all, I hadn't made him happy when I had the opportunity. *Yes, I'll marry you.* I'd lost my chance to say it. I wanted to run to the door, throw it open, fling a different answer down the stairs—but Samira was already there, barraging the empty stairwell with words I didn't think she knew.

"We should have stopped them," Auntie managed, collapsing on the couch with her sobs. "What will your father say? But how could we stop them, we're just women, four women against all their guns. How could we stop them?" Yasmine had crossed the room, taken her mother into her arms, tried to comfort her, all the while tears streaming down her own face.

Samira turned back from her futile task. Anger spent, she said nothing. Not "Shh, it's a mistake, don't worry, don't cry, Baba will sort it out, don't worry, *maalesh*." That was all Yasmine. Samira, she walked across the salon floor and stood in front of me. She didn't offer to help me up from my slumped position on the floor, didn't ask me if I was hurt. I didn't expect it. She looked back at the door for a long time, that white expanse of good-bye, her eyes fixed, her expression unchanging. Then she looked across at me.

# In the Name of God, the Counter, the Reckoner

I can't believe how much has changed. Only a few days, yet it seems forever that we've lived this way.

Nassir moved his cabinet into our room, packed his computer parts in boxes and carted them across town to a friend's house. Now he sleeps on the salon couch. Sarah and Mohammad and Dimah and Mariam have his room, but no one is happy about it. Of course, it's hard to know what Mohammad thinks; he's never around. "People to see, people to see," he says, leaving the house early in the morning and coming home after midnight. I'm not sure whether he's avoiding the relatives who descend on us with pity and cake, or Sarah, who hasn't opened her mouth since they arrived. The only good news: there's no question of Auntie Um Noah moving in now. Where would she sleep? Under the kitchen sink?

Dimah is whinier than I remember: "I want to watch *Sesame Street*, I want my red shoes, I want hamburger for dinner," and since Sarah can't be bothered, it falls to Mama to distract her. Like Mama doesn't have enough to do. Mariam, well, I didn't think she could get worse, but she has. They've been here for only two days and already she's emptied an entire tube of toothpaste, hidden bugs in Nassir's underwear drawer, and broken the television. "I didn't mean it, Auntie, I was spinning around, pretending to be a Powder Puff girl, and I had to destroy everything in my path." And then there's Dimah: "I want to watch (sob, sob) *Sesame Street*."

I know they're small children, and they don't understand why they have to live in a single room in a tiny apartment instead of the six-room palace they had in the Emirates. But even Mama, that paragon of virtue, seems exhausted by it all. She sat down with a heavy thud in the kitchen last night after she'd finally wrestled Dimah into bed and bribed Mariam to sleep with two stories about Juha and his donkey. "I thought boys were harder than girls," she said. "But those two have more energy than all of mine put together. Or maybe I'm too old."

"You're not old," I said. I was scouring the dishes in soapy water, dishes encrusted on both sides with yogurt and beans. Dimah.

"I am. My knees creak when I sit down and my wrists ache when it rains. My favorite songs are sung by Um Kalthum—"

"Everybody's favorite songs are sung by Um Kalthum," I said. I turned to the last bowl, filled with a mixture of orange juice and uncooked rice. Mariam.

"But not so old I don't remember what it's like to be a teenage girl."

The silence stretched between us. Mama doesn't know anything about being a teenage girl, because she never was one. Married at twelve, a mother at thirteen, a grown-up woman with responsibilities at an age when all I worried about was finishing my lessons. She never had this in-between time, this place where a girl can take care of herself but she's not yet required to take care of anybody else. She's not qualified to give me advice.

"I know it must seem like we're all consumed with Mohammad and his problems, but that doesn't mean I don't realize things have been—difficult for you."

She meant Fowzi. Nothing could overshadow the drama of a displaced family quite like an arrest. The news, furtive, whispered, secret, nonetheless spread like malaria. By the time I arrived home that evening, Mama was waiting at the door. She checked me for bruises, cradled me in her arms, stood outside the bathroom as I tried to scrub out the sordid memories with a scouring pad. That first evening, there was silence, and I didn't know enough to be grateful for it.

In a family that has raised gossip to an art form, every minute seems to be filled with some kind of speculation about Fowzi. Most of it unbearable. *Tadmor Prison—that's where they take the political prisoners—out in the desert, you know, underground, they go for months without seeing sunlight.* Or: *My cousin's husband's brother was Brotherhood, they took him at the airport twelve years ago, and no one's seen him since.* Worst of all: *I heard they're handing religious fanatics over to the Americans, shipping them straight to Guantanamo Bay.*

I decided early on not to talk about it. "She was traumatized," I hear Mama explain behind me every time I leave the room. "So tragic, such a thing for a young girl to witness."

Just because I don't say anything, doesn't mean I don't think anything. As I watered Mama's wilted begonia this afternoon, my thoughts spun faster than missile propulsion. My anger at Fowzi, my rage at my own inaction, I put in proper context. That's what they want, isn't it, for us to take it out on each other and let them operate on the margins of civilization? Why shouldn't Fowzi speak out against injustice? Who was I to discourage him? No, my anger was directed at the proper targets now—the men who'd beaten my cousin, the superiors who'd ordered his arrest, the corrupt leaders who'd set up a system that benefits them and nobody else.

I carried Mama's watering can into the bedroom, turning sideways to squeeze past Nassir's cabinet. I took a minute to add some water to the red flowers in an urn on Mama's dressing table, blocking out the noise of my boisterous nieces. Dimah and Mariam were jumping on my bed, counting up to twenty and back down again. How many times had I scolded them since I arrived home from school? Pretending not to see them, I walked out onto the balcony.

Mama had rescued the plant I'd sent flying, but the splintered pot must have been hopeless. She'd replanted it in a wide-mouthed plastic bottle with a Tang label on the side. Next to it, looking just as neglected, a lily drooped inside a rusty pail. I drenched them both with water, and as they opened their faces to the sun, the innocent action seemed to ignite my rage again.

I had bucketfuls left over for whoever had betrayed Fowzi. A traitor who deserved to burn in hell; I hoped God had made suitable plans. Not my place to think about someone else's hereafter, but that was one more thought I couldn't control.

Control. That was what I needed to do, take control. I poured more water on the flowers, their stalks, their stems, their petals. Not enough to drown them, but almost.

More irritating than the constant swirl of whispered conversation that centered around Fowzi was the fact that no one was doing anything about it. They talked about doing things, of course, these macho cousins and uncles of mine. Making phone calls, sidling up to someone's cousin three times removed who's second in command at the department of defense, debating how much it costs to bribe the guards at Tadmor. But nothing happens. "Patience, prayer, and piety," Mama said to me when I exploded in frustration, back before I realized words were futile. "We can't let anger rule our better judgment."

God did not reward the Muslims for waiting in patience while the Unbelievers picked them off one by one, did He? Nor did He reward their Helpers for waiting in piety while the Idolaters ravaged their cities. God helps she who helps herself, she who helps the Muslims.

I left the watering can where it was, on its side, dripping into the garden below. I strode back into the bedroom, barked at my nieces, ordered them out. They scrambled for the door.

Someone has to take control, right? Someone has to help the Muslims.

I've already decided that that someone will be me.

# In the Name of God, the Gatherer

Nowhere to hide.

My cousin Bassam stood up in one fluid motion as I entered the salon. "Good afternoon, Nadia," he said. The just-watered begonia had been whisked away and a bouquet of red and pink roses sat in its place, fresh-faced and well nourished in their crystal vase. "I'm so sorry about everything," he continued, searching my face for something—swollen eyes, reddened cheeks, tears?

I hadn't seen Bassam since that afternoon in the park. Rumor had it that he'd spent the last four days at Auntie Um Fowzi's, and for once, I bet rumor got it right. I could picture him setting up office on Fowzi's couch, feeling important as he rang up all his high-powered connections that went absolutely nowhere.

Did I have to be so hard on Bassam?

"What a tragedy." Bassam filled the silence when I didn't answer him. "Not only for Fowzi, although I can't imagine what he must be going through. But his family, too, I can see what's happened to them. Yasmine hasn't stopped crying, and Samira sits staring out the window all day, and Auntie Um Fowzi, she wanders around like a ghost." Bassam shook his head. "Fowzi's the only son. Without his income . . . ."

Bassam leaned toward me and, for one scary moment, I feared he would take my hand in his. "I can only imagine how awful it must have been," he said. Great imagination, that Bassam. "Over and over again this week, I've cursed myself for leaving early that day."

What would he have done, pulled out his trusty revolver and shot the soldiers dead? Told each of us to grab a limb and carry the bodies out to bury in the park across the street?

Mama bustled into the salon, carrying the ever-present clattering tea tray. "Did you see the flowers Bassam brought?" she asked me.

"It was nothing," said Bassam. "Nadia and I were discussing poor Fowzi . . . ."

He kept talking, but for me, that was it. I pushed back the heavy armchair, leaving marks on the floor. "I'm going to buy the tomatoes for dinner tomorrow—you said yourself, Mama, there won't be any vegetable stands open in the morning."

Bassam rose to his feet almost as quickly as I did. "I'll be happy to get them for you, Cousin. Please, don't disturb yourself."

"Nassir can go," said Mama. "He took the girls downstairs to play in Auntie Um Suheil's garden—I can call him over the balcony."

But I was already sliding my *manteau* over my shoulders. "I'll get the tomatoes," I told them, ignoring Mama and her anxious eyes. "I could use the fresh air, and I'm already up and everything." My feet had marched down the hall before they could say anything else, but as I passed through the door, I heard Mama's half whisper: "Such a traumatic thing for a young girl to witness . . . ."

I headed downstairs and out into the sunlight. My anger at Bassam carried me through the garden, around the back of our apartment building, and into the parking lot. How dare he pity Fowzi? And present himself as some kind of SuperBassam, saving the weak and helpless in his button-down uniform?

Fowzi had more courage in a single eyelash than Bassam had in his whole secular frame.

I crossed with the green light, sparing only a glance at the tomato shop. A group of middle-aged women clustered around it, arguing with the shopkeeper over some bruised eggplant. I'd get better prices at the large market two blocks north anyway. And the trek would give me a chance to walk off my frustrations.

As I trudged up the hill, I was overtaken from behind. A young man in a business suit passed on my left without even a

"pardon me." His cell phone rang just as he stepped in front of me, and he answered it in loud, broken English. English. That made me think of American-living Jalil. Was he the one who reported Fowzi's careless comments to the authorities?

Careless, that's all they were. They weren't treasonous or antigovernment or pro-al-Qaeda. Just an unguarded outpouring of what we all thought. I squelched my suspicions that Fowzi had been up to something. The lie about his ID, the evasive conversations, the blue book swept off the table—all could be explained by fear of the repressive regime. Nothing dodgy enough to warrant soldiers with brutal fists and batons.

A niggling feeling persisted: why would Jalil bother? Unless he was lying about everything, he would go back to the U.S. in a few weeks. Or did he work for the CIA? What would be in it for the CIA, though, to have a random Syrian boy tortured by the local authorities?

Unless Fowzi was al-Qaeda.

I couldn't hold that thought, so I swept on to a more believable possibility. Bassam. Pro-Western, anti-Islamicist, he might have reported Fowzi from conviction, not for personal gain. Had he ever said that Islamicists should be beheaded over in Abbasiyin, with the murderers and rapists? Had he advocated shipping them off to the Americans? I couldn't remember anything so extreme, and I felt a little comforted.

Of course it was Bassam who'd goaded Fowzi in the park, who'd asked the dangerous question. *Are you saying Syria should have an Islamic government?*

Engrossed in my suspicions, I walked right past the entrance to the market and found myself on the edge of the highway. The easiest route home—and the quickest, since Mama would be watching the clock—would take me back to the tomato stand.

I sighed, turned on my heel, and picked up speed. I even ducked under a broken gate and cut through an alleyway. A shortcut I'd taken once with Fowzi—my heart hurt, just a little, as

I remembered him ushering Samira and me past the rickety gate and keeping an eye out for rats.

When a boy appeared in an overhead window and leaned out to call, "Running, dear girl? Then run straight to me," I pretended to spit on his building. Wandering the streets alone, shortcutting through dim alleyways—if I was to be less respectable than my former self, I would have to be tougher, too.

I had almost reached the tomato stand when I saw him. My feet tripped over nothing on the ground and I caught myself just before I fell. Either I'd missed him the last time or he'd just come. There, at the corner, sat a beggar, legs sprawled out, head bent. Not my radical beggar, as I'd first thought, but the everyday beggar, propped against his usual traffic light.

It had been quite convenient, that day of the note, when my beggar came and this one stayed home.

I passed the tomato stand, really running now. The shop owners were bent over their leftovers, packing them into cardboard boxes. Just in front of the light, I drew up short.

He spoke without looking up. "Please, dear lady, for the sake of God, for the sake of the Prophet . . . ."

Twisting my neck, I took in our balcony with one quick glance. No one. Mama and Bassam probably still chatting in the salon, the little girls banished to their bedroom, Nassir out and about. Still, no guarantees. I'd have to speak quickly.

"*Salaam aleikum,*" I said.

"*Aleikum salaam.*"

What to say? Perhaps I should wait until next time, when I'd had a chance to plan out what to ask, consider possibilities, discard the dangerous ones.

But what if there was no next time?

"We missed you the other day," I began. Money barely covered the produce these days, but I had a package of biscuits deep in my purse, and a triangle of cheese, wrapped in silver foil. I dropped both at his feet.

He didn't answer, so I tried again. "I hope you weren't ill."

"Life is nothing but one long illness."

Hmmm. Cryptic. "I gave some money to your replacement," I said. "I hope you got a share of it." I had to be careful, speak in code. Beggars gossip as well as anyone. And the secret police could be anywhere. Give one a cap, a little grunge to the cheek, a pair of frayed pants—and there you had it, a beggar who could pass in any corner of the city.

Meaning, hidden under a couple of innocent sentences. That's what I was looking for.

"I've come into a little extra, too," I said. *Don't think of it as lying, just speaking in code.* "And decided to spend it on, of all things, the movies." I spoke word by word, thinking out my plot as I went along. "Tomorrow. *Bride and Prejudice*, it's playing downtown, in Salheya. Two p.m. I can't believe how much I want to go."

A group of women I didn't know, wearing veils with jeans and makeup, bustled onto the sidewalk. The beggar leaned forward, reached out his hand. "For the sake of God, the sake of the Prophet . . . ." One of the girls stopped to rummage in her purse.

Did I dare be more specific? Did I have a choice? The girl dropped a five-lira coin at the beggar's feet and rushed to catch up with her friends. I took a deep breath. "Your replacement should think about it too. Going to the movies."

The beggar was mumbling something. I leaned in close. ". . . if I see him," he finished. Mumble, mumble, and I missed the first part of his next sentence too. ". . . no place for a girl." The movies? Or the dark underworld of the revolution? "But girls nowadays, they do as they please. No stopping them." He collected the coin and slipped it into his pocket.

I meant to say something else but the light changed and I found myself shuffling across the street.

Had I just made an assignation—or a complete fool of myself? Either way, where were my manners, my shyness?

Locked up in Tadmor Prison.

I looked behind me at the beggar sweeping up, stuffing lira into his pockets, jamming his hat back on his head. Time to go find a corner under some stairs to sleep?

Maybe he was too afraid to stay.

Would he pass on my message? "If I see him," he'd said, but then there was all that grumbling about girls. Of course, he'd finished with, "there's no stopping them." Was that true? If this didn't work, would I take it as a sign from God? Or find another, even more dangerous plan? It scared me that I didn't know the answer.

I climbed the stairs, my heart still racing. No going back now. I took a deep breath and prepared myself to enter the apartment with a secret.

Someone was speaking in the salon, so loudly that he obscured the sound of the door opening. "The more the French campaign against *hijab*, the more Muslim women are going to want to wear it. You have whole groups of Moroccan and Algerian women, who never grew up with *hijab*, who saw it as backward or whatever, but the minute the government tells them they can't wear it, well, that scarf goes on their head." Bassam. It figured.

Someone else answered. A girl's voice, quiet but assured. And Mama must have the ears of an elephant because she met me in the hall before I had undone the top button of my *manteau*. "Where have you been?" she asked.

"I went to get the tomatoes."

Mama raised her eyebrows. "Nadia, I know you're upset these days," she said. "And it's frustrating with so many people crammed into this apartment, but I'm still responsible for you. You can't go off, alone, wandering around the streets of the city. Anything might happen."

Wasn't that what I was hoping for?

"I give you a lot of freedom for a girl your age. I could send Nassir to pick you up after school every day, if that's what I need to do. Is it?" Without looking at her, I finished unfastening my buttons and shrugged out of my *manteau*. In the salon, Bassam droned on about France, the seat of liberty.

"I wasn't wandering around, I was looking for tomatoes. I didn't find any, that's all."

For a minute, I thought she would refuse to let me by. Through the kitchen door, I saw a paper sack on the table, lush red tomatoes rolling out the open end. I bit my lip. Should I tell the truth—the stand was crowded the first time I walked by, closed the second? Then Mama sighed, and I took advantage of it to walk around her. *"Salaam aleikum,"* I said to the visitors as I reached the salon. I would have said more, but I was struck dumb at the sight of the young woman sitting beside Nassir on the couch. Dark blue skirt reaching to her ankles. Long-sleeved blue blouse, collared. Navy blue *hijab* wrapped around her face and carefully covering her ears. A modestly dressed, observant Muslim girl.

My cousin Samira.

# In the Name of God,
## the Just,
## He Who Is Entitled to Do What He Does

"I'm so pleased, Sister. Not that it makes Fowzi's tragedy less painful, but Samira's transformation gives you something to hang on to." Mama's words came from a long way away. I shifted the blanket off my face and squinted in the early-morning light. Mama sat beside the door, her nightgown rumpled beneath her, the phone pressed against her ear.

Where was Samira? Bassam had offered to escort her home last night, but she'd decided to stay over, and bunked down on the couch in our room. I twisted around. Bedsheets hung off the side of the bed, a head-shaped dent imprinted the pillow, but there was no sign of human life.

Mama lowered her voice to a whisper. "Don't look at it that way. What happened to Fowzi helped her put aside frivolous things and follow God's commands."

Was this true? I sat up in bed, wishing I could shake the feeling that Samira had a hidden motive. For months I had wanted her to study Qur'an and cover her head; she finally does and my only response is skepticism? *Please God, help me to believe in Your powers of persuasion.*

"Of course not, Sister." The sound of running water in the bathroom next door drowned out the rest of Mama's words. She cut her conversation short, and had hung up the phone by the time Samira pushed open the door, bundled up in my bathrobe, a towel wrapped around her head.

"I was just talking to your mother, Samira," said Mama.

PAULA JOLIN

"So early?"

Mama swept on. "She thinks—and I agree—that it would be a good idea for the two of you to visit Auntie Um Noah this afternoon."

I groaned. So did Samira, not so eager to feel sorry for Auntie Um Noah now that her own time and comfort were at stake.

"I was going to take the little girls to Salheya, get them ice cream cones," I said. Mama looked at me. I continued, "If you buy those little cones from the corner stands, they're only twenty lira each."

"That's thoughtful, Nadia, but I believe Sarah's taking them out this afternoon," she said at last. "And the Prophet took care to visit his elderly relatives."

That was that.

As if Mama weren't enough, Mohammad chose that morning to play the big, bad brother. I was on the balcony, hanging out laundry, when he came out. "Your behavior will not be tolerated while I am living in this house," he said, without a 'good morning.' "You might have gotten away with murder under weak-willed Nassir, but things are different now."

I wrung out one of his undershirts, careful to drip cold water on his toes. "Excuse me?"

"Don't play innocent, Nadia. I heard all about you wandering the streets alone yesterday. Worse, some of the opinions you've been spouting are far too radical—"

How ridiculous. My opinions were more moderate than those harbored by most of Damascus. I was just less afraid to voice them. "Learning about my religion is radical?"

He continued as though he hadn't heard me. "Your opinions are dangerous, unsophisticated, and—let me tell you—un-Islamic. There's a difference between being pious and being radical. Islam is about kindness, Nadia, about tolerance, about consideration for others. It's not all these rules you're so hung up on, what to wear and when to pray and whether you should shake hands with men or not."

When he was living high in the Emirates, Mohammad wasn't concerned with piety. He and Sarah bragged about their sea-view apartment in Dubai and their company car, a 2002 import in green.

"And I agree with Mama, Nadia, you need to focus more on your schoolwork and less on foreign policies you can't do anything about." He took a deep breath. "I know you're upset about Fowzi's arrest, but I have to say this: it was his own fault, and I would hope you'd learn something—"

Swoosh. Flop. *Smack.* A pair of Mohammad's underwear slipped out of my grasp and danced for a second on the wind before landing in Auntie Um Suheil's garden. Sparkly blue briefs glittered up at us from the dark earth.

"Go and get those," Mohammad snarled.

"I was just going."

"And take a bag with you, so you don't have to carry them in the open."

But I was already gone.

After twenty minutes well spent with Auntie Um Suheil's nieces, breakfasting on fresh oranges and giggling over my brother's barely there underwear, I came home to find that Mohammad had fled. Samira, dressed and waiting, was drumming her feet against the bottom of the couch.

Right. Samira. My chest tightened. What was the chance she would want to go radical-hunting with me today?

Down by the side of the highway a few minutes later, shielding my eyes from the sun, I caught sight of a new billboard across the street. A girl in a white dress, against a background of wild green poppies. I said, "What do you think about window shopping in Salheya? They should have the new fall clothes in."

"Since when do you give a damn about new fall clothes?"

I fiddled with the top button of my *manteau*. "Since it gives me an excuse to put off Auntie Um Noah. Come on—we can look for new scarves for you."

"Not like I could afford one." She shrugged. "But why not?

Any minute without Auntie Um Noah is a good minute."

The bus for Salheya pulled up and I climbed on behind Samira, sidling past the lone rider, a young man fiddling with an enormous cell phone. As we pulled down the seats in the very back, I took advantage of the almost privacy to tug on the end of her *hijab* and say, "So? What about this new style of yours anyway? Mama thinks it's a miracle from God."

"And you don't?" The driver cut a corner—literally, bumping the bus over a curb to take a sharp right—and Samira skittered against me. "You think my religious conversion is some kind of hoax?"

"It's a bit sudden, that's all. After everything you've been saying lately, I'd have been less surprised if you turned up in a bikini."

"You like to think the worst of me, don't you?" She had a point. Holding me upright as the driver steamed through another red light, she added, "No religious conversion—you're right about that. I'm still an Arab feminist, just so you get your facts straight. The Qur'an needs to be reinterpreted by modern scholars, men and women. And for the record, nothing in it says women have to cover their heads."

"Then why are you doing it?"

"It's the best way to say 'fuck you' to a government that could be killing my brother as we speak," she said. The government hates the scarf on a woman's head, proof that allegiance to God is more important than allegiance to the ruling party. A vivid reminder, however silent, however cloaked, that Islamic resentment throbs in every corner of the city.

Still, I didn't know what to say. I'd never heard a girl use language like that before—certainly not a girl I'd grown up with, chased around the backyard, watched tweeze out one entire eyebrow. Then again, it was hardly as shocking as soldiers beating the shit—yes, vulgar language did feel good—out of someone I loved.

The bus roared passed the Central Bank, down the wide

boulevards of downtown Damascus, and then up Maysaloun Street to Hotel Cham. I spotted the theater at the top of the hill. "On the right," I called out in my most professional voice.

I stood up. Samira was still seated, staring out the window. "I'm proud to be a Muslim," she said. "Just not the kind of Muslim who's going to cater to the whim of some stupid man, one perfectly capable of getting up and boiling the rice, or whatever it is, himself."

"The Prophet said, 'If it was permissible for a woman to worship anything other than God, I would order a woman to worship her husband.'"

The minibus rocketed to the side of the road and skittered to a stop. My heart drummed a little staccato beat as I made my way to the front, almost too nervous to look out the window. Would he be waiting for me on the corner, like a boy in a Western movie? Of course not. What would I say to Samira—wait, where was she?

Still in the back of the bus. I whirled around. "Aren't you coming?" The driver beeped the horn and Samira rose to her feet, followed me. I stepped off the bus and onto the crowded sidewalk, trying to look in every direction at once. No beggar boy waiting on the curb, just hoards of people pressing each other ever closer to the shiny theater doors. "Do you really believe that?" asked Samira.

"Believe what?"

"Nadia! We were just having a conversation where you said a woman should worship her husband."

"I didn't say that." Over the heads of the crowd I saw the theater posters: a Jackie Chan kick-up, an American romance, and, there it was, *Bride and Prejudice*. "The Prophet said a woman *couldn't* worship her husband, because it's wrong to worship anything except God."

I fingered the piece of paper in my pocket, small, pink, cut to the size of a fifty-lira note, with the words *More information please* written in English. God helps she who prepares herself.

Samira was shaking her head in something—disbelief? Disgust? I wasn't paying much attention. I was too busy staring at the beggar in front of the theater, the one sitting on the ground, hand held out, head bent over the collection of papers at his feet. Pamphlets—blue, green, yellow—with, yes, Qur'an verses on them. Heart, meet bass drum.

A hot, sharp wind fluttered some of the pages in the basket. Was this my radical? Here in front of the theater where I most—least?—expected him? Or was it someone else? Only one way to find out. I headed toward the corner.

# In the Name of God,
## the Expediter,
## the Promoter,
## He Who Puts Things in the Right Place

Too young. Too much drool. Too much beard on his chin. And too obvious. If the same beggar showed up on every corner of the city, wouldn't the secret police take note?

"Where are you going?" asked Samira, clawing at my arm. "And why'd you tell the driver to let us off here? Now we'll have to walk all the way to the end of the street."

"I thought I saw a girl in my class," I said, scanning the crowd. Mostly men, mostly young, nearly all in jeans and T-shirts. The too-tall basketball types I eliminated right away, the dark-skinned Kurds, the middle-aged guy with the kid on his shoulders. That still left a lot of everyone elses.

Was that him? No, too tall, too skinny, but what about the next one? If he just moved his damn elbow—

Right height, right size, but my beggar didn't have freckles up and down his arm.

Two women in black *abayas* and face veils stepped on my toes and didn't even say "excuse me" as they headed to the shorter, more sedate woman's line. "Where is she?" asked Samira.

Where was who? Oh, right. My friend from school. If I found the radical, I could always say he was her brother. Flimsy excuse, Samira would be sure to see through it, but what else could I say? *Take a good look, and remember that today's insurgents make tomorrow's leaders?*

PAULA JOLIN

I took a deep breath. "She must be inside—if it was even her. No worry, I'll see her tomorrow."

No choice. I had to let Samira drag me down the street then, along a stretch of road bordered on one side by a city fence and honking cars on the other. The perfect place for a private conversation, if only I had someone to talk to. Besides Samira. I allowed myself one last glance over my shoulder. The end of the line was entering the building. No stragglers stood on the corner, staring off into the distance or peering into every passing face.

Samira babbled on about clothes. New A-line skirts from Paris, jeans that had holes where the pockets should be, silver sequined dresses with no sleeves. None of which she could wear, now that she was *mutahajiba*. I didn't point this out, though. It suited me, her doing all the talking.

A pair of old men, one with a white beard, the other with a flowing mustache, came up quick behind us and almost knocked me over. They wore suit jackets over their *galabiyas* and when they passed us, thick accents confirmed their rural origins. Ignoring my almost-fall, Samira prattled on. I caught the end of her sentence: ". . . don't you think?"

"Yes," I said. "I do." She looked at me. "I mean, I do think so."

The old men reached the corner ahead of us and turned right, brushing by another beggar, his head bent, his hand cupped and held out. What if I was wrong, and beggar was the safest disguise? What if—

Except this beggar had only one foot.

"You're looking for a boy, aren't you?"

"Huh?" Two young men on out-of-control bicycles careened down the street, so close that they flicked mud across my *manteau*. From the back, one of the men looked like a larger version of my beggar. I could hear him laughing as he chased the other through the crowd, his long legs hunched up over the bike pedals.

Samira was staring at me. "All this time—I always thought you had a thing for Fowzi."

"Are you crazy?"

"I'm getting out of here." She strode into the street and grabbed the door of a slow-moving cab. "Midan Tahrir," she said to the driver as I scrambled in behind her. He rolled down the window and blew a stream of smoke into the open air by way of an answer.

Executing a sharp turn, he drove half a block down the wrong side of the street and sped off across the city. I snuck a glance at Samira, gripping her armrest on the other side of the cab. Damn. I'd chosen the wrong companion. Yasmine would have been too delirious over the actors in the posters to even notice what I was doing.

On the other side of the cab, Samira sat, back tense, hand gripping the armrest. I opened my mouth to say something and shut it again. Her comment about Fowzi was so embarrassing, so perceptive, I knew I had to answer it, but I didn't. I didn't want to talk about Fowzi. Disappointed over my missed encounter, I didn't want to talk about anything. I sat in silence as our second wild driver of the day managed to run every traffic light until, somehow still alive, we approached Tahrir Square. "Next left," Samira directed. She turned to me as we climbed out: "Nadia, do you have any change?"

I felt in the pockets of my *manteau*—first the left, where I turned up a couple of coins, and then the right, where I met with a flimsy piece of paper. Money? No . . . brown paper, frayed at the edges. What was this? Homework? English letters, but not a book I'd ever read before. *Meet Me at Midnight—Sweet Valley High #124* by Francine Pascal. What on earth? It was the title piece to a book, probably left by some tourist, confiscated by the hotel owner and sold at one of the secondhand bookstands under the White Bridge. Fine. But how did it end up in my pocket? I turned it over. *Noon,* someone had written on the back. *Monday.*

"Nadia? I asked if you had change."

*Midnight.* In Arabic, *Muntasafa al-Layle.* There was a café-restaurant by that name in the ritzy neighborhood of Abu Romani, south of Muhajireen. Where the trendy, Euro-wannabes hang out, in their imported jeans, wafting foreign perfume. Boys with long hair, girls with short skirts. Exactly the kind of place I'd never go.

"I don't have all day," said the driver to Samira, stubbing out his cigarette in the tin tray stuck between the seats.

"Nadia? Change, please."

This couldn't mean anything. Could it? The boys on the bicycle who'd brushed by me, the old men with their funky accents—the veiled "women" who'd almost taken off my toes. Could one of them be my radical?

The driver tapped his fingers against the edge of the window.

"Oh, sorry." I handed her the coins I'd found. She looked at them as though they were currency from Mars. She opened her mouth, then seemed to think better of her next question and tossed the coins through the window, where they fell into the driver's lap. While he sputtered, Samira grabbed my arm and pulled me toward Auntie Um Noah's building.

"That's all you had?" she asked, picking up speed. I stumbled in my heels and swore for the hundredth time that I would switch to flats. "Why didn't you tell me you didn't have any money?"

Behind us, a ragged shout pierced the air, followed by the slamming of a car door. "I thought you had enough," I said.

Samira didn't answer. She ran through the open-air lobby of Auntie Um Noah's building and hit the stairs. No time to think. Footsteps pounded the pavement behind me. I kicked off my heels, scooped them up in one hand, and chased after my cousin.

# In the Name of God,
# the Loving

We burst through Auntie Um Noah's door without knocking. At the bottom of the stairs, someone had stopped the intruder. "Taxi . . . refused to pay . . . *hijabi* hooligans . . . ." The driver's mumbles drifted up the stairs.

"This is a respectable building, no hooligans live here," said another man's voice, growing distant as he escorted the driver out of the building.

Samira shrugged her shoulders and straightened her *manteau*. "Think of all the people he's overcharged in his professional life."

I lifted my feet one at a time and stared at the bottoms of my soiled stockings. Even if he did cheat people, that didn't make our behavior right. Suppressing a guilty twinge, I followed her into the salon. To my surprise, my brother Mohammad occupied the seat closest to the door, sipping tea and arguing with a couple of Auntie's grand-nephews. Something about an international cabal that controlled the Internet. I couldn't be bothered to figure out what side Mohammad was on.

Instead, I kissed Auntie Um Noah on both cheeks and filled her cup whenever she ran out of tea, which seemed to be every five minutes. She had a spirited discussion with Samira about the most fashionable way to wear *hijab*, but I spoke little. "You were such a bright, helpful child," said Auntie Um Noah. "Whatever happened to you?"

The afternoon was more of the excruciating same, until Mohammad finally stood up to leave. After a silent trip home, I climbed out of the cab, but he made no move to follow me. "Aren't you coming?"

PAULA JOLIN

"I'll be home later."

With cramped shoulders and an almost invisible frown, I climbed the steps to our apartment. I sighed and reached to pull our already half-opened door. Strange, Mama wasn't in the kitchen, or the salon. I found her on the balcony, playing with the flat leaves of the parsley plant. "You startled me," she said. "How was Auntie Um Noah?"

"The usual," I said. "She told me I'd been such a kind and jolly child and what on earth had happened to me."

I meant it to be funny, but Mama didn't laugh. "Oh, Nadia." She sighed. "Were you talking politics again?"

I wanted to say something clever, something so adult and profound that it would shame her. But I couldn't think of anything. "What if I was?"

Mama stared down at the leaf. "You didn't used to be like this, Nadia. So hard, so . . . remote."

"Well, things change." Three girls making *kibba* in the kitchen, and then—a mother sobbing, a sister shouting into empty hallways, a cousin gone. Just gone. "Sometimes in an instant."

"I know," said Mama. One more sympathetic, useless "it takes time," and I would have screamed. But she said, "I know what it's like, to have your whole world change in an instant."

Uh-huh. Her life had been pretty even keel: from her father's house to her husband's house, not much room for drama there.

"I was twelve." Mama didn't say anything else for a long minute, just tore another leaf off the plant and held it between two fingers. "You know, I was so young when they came for me, still playing in the street with the other children." I didn't know what she was talking about, not until she added, "I loved the idea of being a bride. I thought, 'Ooh, they're going to dress me up, and I can wear makeup, and everyone will tell me how pretty I am.' I loved being the center of attention. I loved the party, too. Then when it was all over, you know, I didn't understand." There was a long pause, and I found myself backing up, bracing my shoulders against the screen door. "I wanted to go home with my mother. They told me—you have to stay here now, you live here, he's your husband. And I cried."

I did not want to know this.

"He lived with his father then, in an Arabic-style house, out in Masaken Barza. The party was in the courtyard, and the women carried me into his room."

I cleared my throat to change the conversation, but nothing came out.

"We were all so innocent," she went on. "You girls with your biology classes and your foreign movies, you have some idea of the—the relationship between a husband and wife, but my parents, they didn't even sleep in the same room. My mother said nothing to me the night before, and I'll never forget the first time I saw him there."

She put the leaf on the balcony railing and it sat there, crumpled, until the wind blew it off. "He was older than me, of course, much older, but he was religious, and he had no experience either. I remember looking at him, standing there, in the light of the candle, and listening to him explain that he was going to stick . . ." She paused. "Stick it in my most private place. I was so scared. That big thing in this tiny place? He's going to break me in two, I thought, he's going to break me in two."

I finally managed to say something. "Mama, do you want some tea?"

She smiled—a tight smile—and gripped the rail with both hands. "No, thank you, Nadia. I didn't mean to embarrass you. I just . . . well, as you can imagine, after that things were very different."

I nodded. I couldn't help imagining it, no matter how hard I tried. "I'm going to make some tea for me; I'll bring you a cup," I said, and escaped to the kitchen.

When I returned, I found her cleaning the screen door with a soapy rag, and I balanced her tea on the nearest chair. "Time to hit the books," I mumbled, retreating to the bedroom, closing the door tight behind me. The house, usually so full of Mariam's pranks and Dimah's laughter, was strangely silent now. I could study if I wanted to, I thought as I sat behind my tiny desk, crammed into the corner. But I didn't. I took out *Meet Me at Midnight* and stared at it one more time.

In the Name of God,
the Compassionate


Midnight.

The time, not the restaurant. I couldn't sleep. I kept hearing the announcer on al-Jazeera. *United States aircraft bombed a wedding party in Iraq, five miles from the Syrian border. Dozens were killed.* The smiling faces of the Iraqis gathering for the wedding party, the bride climbing out of a white pickup truck, juxtaposed with exploding bombs, piercing screams. *"Ya Allah!"*

"I can't watch this anymore," Mama said, and headed for the balcony.

I wanted to call after her, *Let the devil into the room and see what happens!* but I stopped myself. She's not the head of an Arab country who accepted U.S. aid and everything that comes with it. She's not the author of one of those "Islam means whatever you want it to" books. She's not even a Westoxified American supporter, who tears off her scarf and bathes in mixed company.

She's like me, really, only born before her time.

I watched the news coverage of the Iraqi wedding for hours. So it's funny that, when I wake up at midnight, it's not that wedding that's replaying itself in my head, but one I've never seen. My grandfather's house in Masaken Barza is lit with candles because the electricity is so unreliable. Women arrive early, faces hidden behind black veils, even their footsteps subdued. Boys and young men lounge around outside, smoking contraband cigarettes and drinking Pepsis, hoping to catch a glimpse of ankle under a passing *abaya*. The bride arrives. Praying that her dress doesn't tear, she eases herself out of the long black car, accompanied by a trail of ululating women and rifle shots.

Dancing all night long. Most of the other women are older, some much older, and they make cheeky jokes the bride cannot understand. She smiles, though, pleased that everyone is watching her, pleased at the compliments on her dancing. "I can dance American," she tells them, and flings herself into a kind of wild disco, finger pointing upward, legs kicked in the other direction.

Fine. I made that part up.

But not the rest of it. Not the moment when my father walks in the room, and he's naked and enormous and she's a child and scared. I can't stand to think of it. I can't. But I do. She is already hurting down there, from the waxing and cleaning and perfuming. In the old days—was thirty years ago the old days?—they used to draw a circle around the vagina to make sure the man knew the right hole. Because they were all so innocent. Poked and prodded, petted and perfumed, served up like lamb to the slaughter . . . .

How could she have loved my father after that?

Maybe she didn't. I remember her at the funeral: she wore black and cried long tears and eventually had to be sedated. She stayed home the requisite forty days and nights, and never complained, not once, and ate almost nothing. We had to cajole her with her favorite fruits, cherries and strawberries and tomatoes. But I was young, just going on nine, and I couldn't remember before that. Certainly there was no romance, like the movies, holding hands or snuggling in each other's laps or candlelit dinners while they sent us to the babysitter. That never bothered me, though. I thought they loved each other in a more dignified, Islamic way.

*I remember looking at him, standing in the light of the candle, and listening to him explain that he was going to stick it in my most private place.* Couldn't get more dignified than that.

I turned the pillow over and crushed my cheek into the cool underside. Maybe I was overreacting. Thinking like an Unbeliever. The Prophet had married Aisha when she was nine, hadn't he? Straight from toys to wifehood, and the most celebrated woman in Muslim history, honored for her role in creating a tradition of the Prophet's life followed by a billion-plus people today. Girls matured faster then, though, we learned that in biology. A girl of nine then was like a girl of eighteen, even twenty, today.

*I was twelve.*

*Go to sleep, Nadia.* I flipped over on the bed. Flat on my back, staring up at the ceiling, I found the picture of a child bride in the shadows there. Shawl tumbling off her shoulders, legs kicking up in a cancan, face blank. Think about Iraq, Nadia. Think about the evil Americans, killing thirteen children because they couldn't read their intelligence reports properly. Think about—

*That big thing in this tiny place.*

Across the room I heard her even breathing, her light snores. I sat up in bed. I was being ridiculous. Wasn't I? I knew she'd married young, married at twelve even. Knew, though I'd never thought about it, that she'd had marital relations then. Mohammad was born before her fourteenth birthday. So what was different now?

I'd never known she minded.

I should have. When I crested puberty, she laughed away the aunties who suggested matches for me. "You were a married woman by this age," they'd said, and then, "A big girl like this, don't waste her beauty, you'll regret it." My always-polite mother smiled as though they were telling jokes, and said, "Nadia's going to university. When she's done and has a job and is about twenty-five years old, then will be the time to think of marriage."

Once I asked her, "If that's what you want for me, why didn't you go to university yourself?" We were on the balcony, I remember; it was fall and leaves were dropping to the ground. Bits of yellow and red had rained on our feet. An earth science textbook was open on my knees, and she had some brightly colored yarn strung on needles between her hands. "My family was, well, they were quite conservative," she said at last. "And things were different then. Only rich girls went to school past sixth year. For the rest of us, reading and adding up, that was enough." A few minutes later, she left with her knitting and came back with a book. *Crime and Punishment,* by Dostoevsky. "If I'd gone to university," she said, "I would have studied literature."

"Only people who aren't smart enough to study science study literature," I told her.

*Think about something else, Nadia. Count to five in all the languages you know. Wahad, ithnane, thalatha, arbaa, khamsa. One, two, three, four, five. Un, deux, trois, quatre, cinq. Think about your beggar boy. Meet Me at Midnight, Monday, Noon. I'd have to skip school. Of course, I wasn't going . . . .*

I flopped over on my stomach again. In this dream he had light hair and sapphire eyes and he was saying, "They'll be telling stories about the brave, never-look-back Arabian princess Nadia in the cafes of Damascus for decades to come . . . ."

And that's the last ridiculous thing I thought about before I fell asleep.

# In the Name of God, the Firm One

Friday, Saturday, Sunday. Each day hotter than the last. As usual, spring leapfrogged over us and dove headfirst into summer. In the stale air puffed around the apartment by the corner fans, I didn't think about that stupid assignation at all. Well, maybe once. Or twice. Fine, three times. First thought: *This is what you asked for, Nadia.* And then: *I never meant him to really show up.* Finally: *God, protect me from unproductive ideas.* I always added: I'm not going.

Sunday night, just before bed, I made ablutions and prepared to pray *istakhara*, the decision prayer. I sank to my knees, lips murmuring, *"O God! I seek Your guidance by virtue of Your knowledge, and I seek ability by virtue of Your power, and I ask You of Your great bounty."* Look to the right, look to the left. *"You have power, I have none. You know, I know not. You are the Knower of hidden things."*

I bent over, lowered my head to the ground, prostrated myself before my Creator. *"O God! If in Your knowledge, this meeting is good for my religion, my livelihood and my affairs, immediate and in the distance, then ordain it for me, make it easy for me and bless it for me."* I rose to my knees, pressed my hands together. *"And if in Your knowledge, this meeting is bad for my religion, my livelihood and my affairs, immediate and in the distance, then turn it away from me, and turn me away from it."* I was back on my feet, feelings of peace and certainty flooding through me. *"And ordain for me the good wherever it is and make me pleased with it."*

I climbed beneath the sheets I'd cooled in the freezer for an hour. Tiny drips of ice water snaked across my bare arms and legs. *Why were you worrying, Nadia?* God is the best of planners.

Plans. What kind of plans did God have for my future? As I closed my eyes, I expected to picture a college classroom, wedding gold, maybe a baby. Instead I saw a dark-haired, dark-eyed young man sitting in a fashionable café, bent over a stack of papers. The top page faded out a little and then came into focus. *A Manual for a Mutiny*, I read. And underneath it: my name.

The results of my *istakhara* prayer haunted me through breakfast the following morning and all the way to school. Not every prayer turns out right; the solution is to try again. If only God had been more clear.

I shifted the backpack resting below my shoulders as I joined the queue of girls streaming into the school building. Down the tiled hallway, boots stomping against the floor. Did they have to sound so final?

Our usual orderly classroom was in an uproar. Girls chattered and squealed, admired each other's scarves, copied lessons. One stood at the very edge of the doorway and tried to toss wads of paper through the window on the far side of the room. "What luck," she said to me. "Miss went with her family to pick up her brother at the airport. She won't be in till afternoon."

Sign number three. Just in case I was stubborn enough to ignore the certainty sent by God, and the images in my head after I prayed *istakhara*. Up and down the hallway, students were filing into their classrooms, teachers regaining order with sharp raps to their chalkboards. Any minute now, the principal herself would come to subdue our room.

*Seize the day, Nadia.* I seized. I backed out of the classroom, mixed into the crowd, hit the steps running. Was that a faint voice calling, "Nadia, where are you going?" If so, I didn't hear it. Through the courtyard, through the gate—then I turned the corner and, thankfully, outran the wind.

I took a crosstown bus and headed to the Hafez al-Assad Library, where I spent the morning in peace. At 11:20 I slipped into the bathroom and proceeded to change my clothes. *Manteau* and calf-length cotton skirt went in the backpack. Blue jeans came out. I rolled up the sleeves of the red blouse I'd worn—a clue, had my mother seen it, since I never wear that blouse to school—and unbuttoned the top button. In the mirror, Bassam's crescent necklace shone against my skin.

Makeup. My hand shook as I applied the lipstick, eye shadow, blush I'd borrowed from Mama's collection, reserved for fancy wedding parties. A librarian came into the bathroom and scolded me with disapproving eyebrows. She thought I was on my way to meet a lover. For a moment, I felt disgraced. Was I crazy? A seventeen-year-old girl, thinking the secret police are tracking her, trying to throw them off her scent with bits of color and an old pair of jeans. Then I saw Fowzi's thin face, scarred and bruised, dribbling blood. My mouth straightened into a thin line as I added lip gloss. Good. If she thought I was meeting a lover, maybe everyone else would, too.

I raised my hand to my *hijab*. The first day of my thirteenth Ramadan, I'd come down to breakfast with it over my head, tight on one side, loose on the other. I hadn't quite gotten the hang of the pins yet. "Are you sure?" asked Mama, a worried look on her face. "There's plenty of time for you to grow up."

"It feels right, Mama," I said. Not only right, it felt adult, and special. No one would laugh at me if I wanted to wear high-heeled shoes, and even Nassir had to take care with me. "Let me see where my sister is," I'd hear him call out to his friends, making them wait by the door while he ensured I was comfortably out of sight. "She's *mutahajiba* now."

Over the years, *hijab* had become more than a piece of cloth. It was my right to privacy and protection. Put on a head scarf and I feel invincible, armored with God's love and approval. I belong to myself and no one else. My hair, my body: my private property, not an opportunity to feast for every passing man. Sometimes I feel so sorry for non-Muslim girls, not allowed to cover their hair, forced to perform for men like trained seals, no private space to be themselves.

I left the *hijab* in place. Plenty of chic, Westernized, boyfriend-having girls wear *hijab* and makeup. Try to have it both ways. Like me, as I left the library and headed up the steep hill toward Abu Romani. Wanting to be a *jihadi* and transgress the laws of God all at the same time.

It took me twenty-five minutes to reach *Muntasafa al-Layle*. It was in a tiny courtyard, ringed by other fashionable restaurants. A gaggle of girls stood outside, gossiping, every third word they said English or French: "—you know . . . like . . . *comme ca.*" Not one of them had a scarf on her head. I gritted my teeth, pushed my *hijab* back a few inches. Then I took a deep breath, recited the *shahada* very, very softly—"There is no God but God and Mohammad is His Prophet"—and marched past the girls.

I pushed open the door to the restaurant. The air-conditioning hit me hard in the face. What on earth was I doing? Shiny tables made for two, immaculate counter, waitstaff in matching uniforms. They'd know in a minute, from my ragtag clothes—jeans with the worn knees, red blouse that looked fine in the mirror at home—I didn't belong here. "Excuse me." I swung around, half expecting a bouncer to throw me out. But the voice came from a young man sitting by the door. "It's good of you to meet me." He stood up, reaching out a hand as though he knew me.

In a frightening moment of revelation, I saw myself through his eyes: painted, half-*hijab*bed floozy, setting up secret meetings with a strange man. I met his eyes, wide and brown and not innocent. Then I turned and fled.

Out through the automatic door, past the West-obsessed girls, around the corner, up a small hill. Only a few feet to safety. "Nadia!" He caught up with me as my hands gripped the top of a small fence. "Nadia," he said again. He wasn't even breathing hard.

Nothing to tell him but the truth. "I came in disguise," I said.

"Of course you did." He wasn't looking at me; he was looking at the ground. *Say to the believing men that they should lower their gaze and guard their modesty, that will make for greater purity for them* . . . . He put his hand over his heart. "I'm sure you understand, sister, that I don't shake hands with women. My religion."

I stared at him. No lowered gaze from me, at least not until I recovered myself.

"I'm Walid," he said. "A friend of Fowzi's."

A friend of Fowzi's. My grip on the fence relaxed. Those words were my final, my most important sign.

In the Name of God,
the Able,
the Capable,
the One Attributed with Power

"In normal times," said Walid as we walked along the side of the road, a respectable distance between us, "I would never dream of approaching a girl in this way. I believe in the Islamic ideals of courtship and marriage. There's no place in an Islamic society for friendships between men and women. In normal times.

"However, I think you'll agree, the times we live in now are extraordinary."

I flickered my eyelids, a kind of assent. Walid had turned his back while I fixed my *hijab* and, despite the makeup still staining my face, I felt more myself. "You've been following me," I told him, determined to get at least some of my questions answered. "How do you know Fowzi anyway? And what do you want with me?"

"Not following you, not exactly." He smiled. "After all, *Bride and Prejudice* wasn't my idea, was it? A clever one, though I wish you had better taste in movies."

Before I could defend my choice, he led me around the low fence to reach the residential road and gestured at the nearest side street. "Let's take that. If we follow it to the end, it links up with the highway leading to the mountain. There shouldn't be many people walking there." We crossed fresh black pavement, uninterrupted by a single car. Brick walls lined both sides of the small street, protecting the privacy of those who lived behind them.

"The first night I saw you, you probably don't remember. It was the night the police stopped you."

"You were drunk."

"Not drunk. Playing a role." Walid reached out his left hand and ran it along the wall as we walked. "We were supposed to meet up that night, but Fowzi's cousin's truck broke down, or else he got spooked. I wasn't sure what was going on, so I checked out a couple of strategic places and one of them paid off. I wanted Fowzi to be prepared."

"Prepared for what?"

Walid waited until the brick wall ended and we walked by an open lot, and then waited again until a passing car took a left at the next stop sign. Still he chose his words with care. "I didn't want a policeman with a good memory to see Fowzi's identity card that night." We came to the end of the side street. "Up or down?" Walid asked me.

"But what happened?" Sharia Nehru stretched for miles in both directions. Down fell sharply, then flattened into a rotary circle with roads branching into town and out to the diplomatic neighborhood of Mezzah. Up wound around twice before disappearing into the mountains. I jerked my head that way.

Walid matched his steps to mine and we passed a pair of elaborate, villa-style houses. The sun, which hadn't seemed hot when I left the schoolgirl queue, settled into a scorching position directly overhead. My shoulders ached with the weight of my backpack. Houses behind us, Walid said, "Nothing happened. But something could have, and I wanted to warn Fowzi that there were policemen roaming the streets."

"Something did happen. Fowzi was arrested." With sudden force, I was angry. They had been played for fools, the two of them, or the group of them, or whoever they were. Now Fowzi was paying for it with his life.

Walid stopped on the rocky sidewalk. He reached into the pocket of his striped blue-and-white shirt and pulled out a miniature Qur'an, the tiny version some girls wear in gold cases around their necks. "I swear to you, Nadia, Fowzi's arrest had nothing to do with us." The Qur'an rested between his thumb and forefinger alone but that simple touch made his word more binding, more certain, than if squeezed out of him by slipping a hood over his head and attaching electrical wires to his private parts. "I swear to you in the name of God."

We resumed walking, more slowly this time. My face felt itchy, the result of makeup smeared with sweat. My backpack grew heavier and more uncomfortable with every step. "Someone betrayed Fowzi," said Walid. "And when I find out who it was. . . ."

I didn't want to talk about more violence. "But you started following me before Fowzi was arrested."

"I wasn't following you. I recognized you from the night of the police, and when I saw you in Yarmuk with Fowzi's sisters, I was surprised. It didn't seem like your kind of place."

"You didn't tell Fowzi?"

He stepped around a patch of gravel. The trickle of perspiration he wiped off his forehead didn't make him look disheveled but somehow powerful, as though he could defeat anything, including the heat. "I wondered about you, right from the beginning. From what he's told me, Fowzi's sisters are not the—they're not all that aware of the political needs of the Muslims. But you, somehow I knew you were different."

"I try to walk the straight path," I said, a little primly, not sure whether he was making fun of me or not. "I think that God gave us minds and hearts to worship Him. In His infinite mercy, He gave us Islam. Humanity couldn't have asked for a better, kinder, more useful gift."

Walid looked me in the face for the first time. "Do you believe that it's our responsibility, as Muslims, to do everything in our power to establish Islamic law, to implement its justice?"

"I do."

We came to a three-way fork in the road. One route led west

to the suburb of Doumar, the second headed straight up the steep mountainside, and the third took travelers back into Damascus. This time Walid didn't ask me which way. "I knew it," he said instead. "Fowzi didn't want to discuss it with you, but I convinced him. He said he talked to you about it, but you turned him down, said you were too young."

"Fowzi never said anything to me about fighting for a revolution." Walid wasn't making sense. *Think, Nadia.* A stifling spring afternoon, the scent of jasmine, a buzzing bee. *I've been meaning to ask you something, Nadia.*

How stupid I'd been. Fowzi hadn't been proposing marriage, but something quite different. My face, hot with embarrassment, would have given me away if Walid had glanced in my direction. Instead, he swept on. "There are a lot of ways you would be useful, places a modest young woman could go, questions she could ask, things that would be immediately suspect if a man did them." He misinterpreted my still-embarrassed silence. "They only think young girls are less radical because they don't know their own history. Aisha, Hafsa, dozens of others fought side by side with the Believers. They were as fierce and faithful as any Muslim warrior, and earned their place in heaven, may God be pleased with them."

"May God be pleased with them," I echoed.

"Walk to the end of this road, take a right, and you should find a taxi." He took out his wallet and offered me a hundred-lira note, careful to hold just the ends so I could take it without touching his hand. I raised my head and clicked my tongue no. Walid reached behind me, unzipped the pocket of my nylon backpack, and stuck the bill inside. "You're one of us now," he told me.

That was all of his good-bye. He walked down the hill, quick and graceful, growing smaller with every step.

I blinked twice and then he was gone.

# In the Name of God, the Wise, the Judge of Judges

Fowzi's arrest hadn't wrought much change in Yasmine. More subdued dress, perhaps—long sleeves, modest collar— but her eyes still sparkled and her conversation never touched on serious topics. As she and Samira helped me with the dishes after dinner—we'd had a full house, Nassir, of course, and Mohammad's family, in addition to the three of us and Mama—she chattered on about her mother, who'd finally started eating but still wouldn't leave the house. "One of us has to sit with her; Baba's out all day, going from ministry to ministry, trying to find some answers."

From the back of the apartment, I heard Mohammad and Sarah get the girls ready to spend the evening with her mother. I tried not to notice that Mohammad seemed to yell at his wife more than his daughters. "If you had trained them properly, then there wouldn't be all this fuss, would there?" The door slammed. Peace.

Every dish put away, we ventured into the salon, where we found Nassir, his head buried in the bottom drawer of the TV stand. He emerged with a pack of cards. "Forty one, anybody?"

Mama called out, settling down to her embroidery, and no one took my meager excuse about lessons seriously. "You have time for one game, Cousin," Samira said.

Nassir had already shuffled and started dealing, two at a time. "Still can't get over that wedding," he said. "Shocking."

Wedding. I couldn't look at Mama, but then I couldn't not.

She rocked placidly in her chair, clicking her silver needles. She didn't look tragic.

"So ironic," said Samira. "People usually send up fireworks to celebrate their marriages and look what happened here."

"I heard the bride and groom were both dead," said Yasmine. Disapproving clucks all around.

Cards on the table, I picked up my hand. Couldn't Nassir have given me something higher than ten? And why so many spades?

Nassir spoke again. "Some people used to say the wedding ends with the bridegroom wishing he was dead . . . but that seems so, I don't know, horrific now."

"The bridegroom?" asked Samira. "I think it's the bride who wishes she was dead. Cousin Anisa said once she saw her husband's bare feet, that was it for her. She got used to them eventually, though."

"I read a funny joke about that on the Internet, about a woman who liked everything about her husband except his feet . . . how did it go . . .?"

Nassir trailed off. When it became clear he wasn't going to finish, Yasmine leaned forward. "Speaking about the Internet, Nassir, I wanted to ask you something. Do you have any books about Windows 2000?"

Nassir started some incomprehensible answer about how Windows is an operating system, not the Internet. I shifted my cards around and still had a rotten hand. "What do you want computer books for?" I asked Yasmine.

"Oh," she said. She looked a little shy. "I signed up for classes at the institute. English and computers, twice a week."

"Nice," Nassir said, scoring big with a queen.

"Bassam advanced me the money for the courses," she continued. "Strictly a loan, of course. Still, he's so kind. There's no guarantee I'll make the money back. But to get by in anything these days, you need English and computers, especially if you want to go abroad." She jumped a little. Was that Samira who kicked her under the table?

If so, she segued in smoothly, "Abroad or home, everybody needs to know these things. Employers everywhere are looking for the same real-world skills."

"Uh-huh." I should have managed more enthusiasm. I knew it even before Mama looked up with a pained expression, but I just couldn't find any.

Samira tapped the back of her cards with her long fingernails. "I'd have thought you'd be all for it, you're so pro-education."

"I think it's great," I said. I did. "The thing is, when people are dying in Iraq and Palestine, should we really be devoting ourselves to anything else? Maybe we should put all our intellectual resources into getting the infidels off our land."

Of course, Muslims need Muslim doctors, my ambition since Dr. Huda came to speak to our third-year class in her *hijab* and lab coat, stethoscope around her neck. But finding a cure for diabetes wasn't going to chase the Israelis out of Palestine.

No one argued with me, and another round of cards went down to Samira in silence. She stacked them in a small pile at her elbow and then stared hard at her hand, pulling out first one card and then another.

Muslim engineers could build Muslim tanks and guns, so the argument went. But we'd been training Muslim engineers since independence and where had it gotten us? Half of them fled to the West and helped make foreign weapons for the infidels. The others languished in underfunded laboratories with broken equipment. Not one of them had the impact of an uneducated boy in a crowded market with a bomb in his hands.

"Nadia, I thought you were out of diamonds. You played six of clubs in the last diamond round." Nassir's angry voice recalled me to the game. Six of diamonds on the table in front of me, two of diamonds in my hand. Oops.

A sharp rap sounded against the front door, saving me from

having to defend myself. "That's Bassam," said Yasmine, her face a little flushed. "I'd know his knock anywhere." She jumped up to let him in. Nassir tried to sneak a look at her cards but Samira swatted his hand away.

Bassam came into the room, pressed and starched as always. *"Salaam aleikum,"* he said, kissing Nassir on both cheeks. He stepped back, exchanged kisses with Mama, and let her go before he said, "I hear there's someone in this room keeping secrets."

Secrets? My hand, extended in welcome, began to shake. I hoped I looked as innocent as Samira and Yasmine.

"Don't blush, Cousin. I saw you in Abu Romani the other day. Last place I would have expected to find you, so I investigated a little."

Busted.

# In the Name of God,
## the First,
## He Whose Existence Is Without Beginning

Blood rushed into my ears. I waited for Bassam to comment on the blue jeans I'd been wearing in public, my half *hijab*, my—oh God, had he seen me with Walid? No, he wouldn't confront me about a boy in the open like this. Bassam could be discreet. He'd pull Mama aside, deliver the bad news in a horrified whisper, let her handle things. Still, how would I explain a trek to the other side of the city when I was supposed to be sitting quietly in school?

It was a minute before I understood what Samira was saying. "Mama told you!"

Bassam was laughing, shaking my hand, moving on to the next cousin. "Your Mama heard about my visa to America—"

"You got it?" That was Nassir, but we all ignored him.

"And she kept asking me and asking me about going abroad, and I prodded her, and finally she broke down and told me the whole story."

He looked at us like we were all supposed to know what he was talking about. Of course, I was relieved that I was still respectable, but it was annoying to find myself so far out of the gossip rounds. "What story?"

"Samira's going to Geneva," said Yasmine. The words came out in a rush, as though she'd been holding them back all evening.

"Well, not exactly," said Samira. She sat back down at the table and the rest of us negotiated four people for three chairs. I insisted Bassam play my cards. "You can't do worse with them than I have," I said. "Not a single trick so far. And really, I have to study, I haven't even started my physics lesson."

They settled down one after the other, and Bassam frowned at the pair of deuces left in my hand. "Geneva?" reminded Mama from her corner.

"I'm thinking about it, that's all. There's a UN internship for third world women next year—they're looking for young women, aged eighteen to twenty-two, especially from Arab countries. The focus is on women in peace and war." She looked at Mama over her cards. "It would be an amazing opportunity."

Nassir threw out the ace of clubs and the next round began. With a kind of good-bye nod, I stepped into the bedroom and closed the door gently behind me. I tried to imagine Samira *hijab*bed and prayerful in Geneva. I couldn't. Instead I saw her, dark hair flowing over her shoulders, sitting in mixed groups in cafés and calling for women's liberation in a loud voice. Of course, Samira had to make her own decisions. Still, abandoning Islam— that path led straight to hellfire. Not what I wanted for my cousin. Not what I would have predicted the first day I saw her with a scarf. And what could I do about it? Once again, Western values were intruding into my world and I was powerless to stop them.

I found my physics book on my desk, under a pile of papers and notebooks. I left it there. Instead, I grabbed a notebook and a nearly empty fountain pen, and curled up on the bed. *Possibilities* I scrawled across the top of the page.

In the next room, someone collected all the cards and shuffled them. From her corner, Mama said, "Is all this going abroad really necessary, Bassam? You have such a good job in the Gulf."

"Well, it's not a settled thing that I'm going, Auntie. The friend who's arranging my paperwork said it's all clear sailing on their end. But there's still a formal interview here, and maybe some more papers to file. It'll be a while yet."

I wrote, *#1 Identify and reach out to people who've come to Syria to help the Iraqis. Try to raise funds for them.*

Yasmine's long fingernails tapped against the back of her cards. "Is that the guy we met in the park the other day, what was his name, Jalil?" *#2*, I wrote. *Posters. Parks, movie theaters, city walls.* "Because didn't you say he might stay here? That he has friends in high places now?"

I stopped writing in the middle of the page. Friends in high places?

"If he decides to stay here, let me know," said Nassir. "I'll take his job in the States."

I could feel Mama's disapproval from the next room. "You can make more money in the Gulf. Make your money, get out, come home. The people who go to Europe never come back." I noticed she didn't say anything about Samira's proposal.

"Not Europe, Mama. America."

"It's the same thing," she said. "All those Western countries are the same."

"No, they're not," Bassam told her. Someone collected the cards from the table and began shuffling again. "The European countries hate Arabs. Look at the *hijab* laws in France. America's not like that."

"But your children will grow up with colored hair and nose rings, listening to that crazy music that makes them bang their heads against the wall."

"I wouldn't go," said Bassam. "Unless I was married. To a girl who's strong in her religion and strong in her personality, so she can kick me back to the straight path any time I'm about to wander off. A girl who's willing to live abroad, but never forgets that she's Syrian."

"Looks aren't important to you?" asked Yasmine. There was a strange teasing note in her voice. "Are you sure you're a man, and not a plant?"

"The girl I'm thinking of," said Bassam, "she's very pretty. Rest assured of that."

I stretched out my foot and snapped the door shut. Who

wanted to listen to their conversation anyway? I had more important things to do. *#3 Newsletter. #4 A network of itinerants, people like beggars, gypsies, the women from the countryside who sell Marlboro cigarettes.* I got to *#5—underground radio*—before I ran out of ink. I was scrabbling around the desktop for at least a stubby pencil when Samira knocked on the door and poked her head in.

"We broke up the game," she said. "Bassam decided he was hungry and you know Nassir, he can always eat. So Yasmine and I are heading home."

A quick shove of the notebook under my physics book and it was safe.

I walked Samira and Yasmine down the hallway. Outside the sweep of the door, at the edge of the welcome mat, we found flowers, pale blue and bound with a rubber band. "Interesting," said Samira, her voice too low for her sister to hear as we stooped together to pick them up. "From that guy you were looking for the other day?"

"There is no guy," I said. The irritated note in my voice came out perfect. "It's some kind of marketing stunt." I flashed the bright pink paper at her. *Tishreen Park Floral Designs.* Sure enough, an identical bundle sat on the stoop across the hall. "If you don't want them, I'll take them," said Yasmine, holding out her hand. "A bit straggly, but they're still pretty."

I put the flowers into her outstretched palm and listened as my cousins chattered their way down the stairs. My eyes were still on the pink slip of paper Yasmine had left behind. *100 Thursday* read the address on the order form. *Northern Side Gate.*

Time, date, and match to Walid.

# In the Name of God, the Forbearing, the Clement

For a moment, it looked as though Miss wasn't going to buy my explanation about a dentist's appointment. Then she nodded and scrawled her name on a permission-to-exit slip. I raced through the schoolyard, handed the crumpled paper to the guards at the gate, and was out into the street and around the corner before they had a chance to read it.

The first minibus pulled away from the curb before I reached the stop. I squeezed onto the second, packed with men shouting into their cell phones, and breathed a sigh of relief. Until it broke down three blocks from the park entrance. Not bothering to worry about signs from God, I tumbled down the rickety front steps and ran.

1:05. The side entrance was empty. Inside the gate, three teenage boys in jeans and T-shirts kicked around a limp football. A pair of middle-aged foreigners walked through, carrying umbrellas and speaking what sounded like German. Umbrellas. In the midst of summer heat. I looked up to check the sun, only to find it obscured by clouds.

What to do now? Wait? Maybe 1:00 meant 1:15 or 1:30. Maybe Walid had been delayed, doing whatever it was he did. Either way, a young girl could hardly stand in front of a park gate alone.

The football flew over the head of one of the players and he turned around to chase after it, his baseball cap askew, his jeans splattered with mud. "Hey, guys," he called out over his shoulder.

"My sister's here. Gotta run." Ignoring the football, he loped around the edge of the grass and stopped in front of me. "Good afternoon, Nadia," said Walid. *"Salaam aleikum."*

*"Aleikum salaam,"* I managed through my surprise. Millions of questions, yet again. I asked the most innocuous one. "Do you know those guys?"

His eyes flickered back toward the two football players. The ball slipped through the legs of the shorter player and his opponent yelled, "Goal!" "Not at all," said Walid. "Football's useful that way—just jump in anywhere and play the game."

I stole a quick glance at Walid. Despite his jeans and T-shirt, he wasn't the teenager I'd mistaken him for. His face was all hard planes and angles, sharp nose, determined chin, decorated with a bit of overnight stubble.

"Shall we start?" he asked. The gardens at Tishreen were beautiful in their early summer glory. Pink and purple roses lifted wanton faces to the midday sun, green grass sashayed to the beat of God's breeze, the scent of jasmine enticed us onto a tree-lined path.

Not to worry, I told myself as we headed into the wooded area. Walid wasn't that kind of boy. Man. Once we had put enough space between ourselves and the open park, once the boys' shouts had faded, I rummaged through my purse. I drew out a piece of multifolded paper and opened it. Walid wasn't going to have everything his own way.

"What's that?" he asked. Was that a smile in his voice?

"A list I made. Things we can do."

"Things we can do?"

The rocky path crunched and crumbled beneath my high heels. "Well, we're in agreement that things need to change, right? The question is how." I took a deep breath. Would he think my ideas were stupid? "I know that we need to be careful, but I thought that maybe we could start with something like a newspaper. Just a few sheets of paper, linking revolution to Islam."

There, it was out. "We could leave it in key places around the city, where people could find it. Or maybe have beggars, or people who look like beggars, pass it out with their Qur'an leaflets."

Why wasn't he saying anything?

"I mean," I went on, "I mean it could look like leaflets, but it would actually be our paper."

"Nadia," said Walid. The path in front of us forked to the left and right, and our footsteps stopped at the same moment, as though neither of us knew which way to go. "How long do you think it would take the government to figure out who was printing that newspaper?"

The stalwart tree in front of me swayed in the breeze.

"If we distributed the paper in the morning, they'd round up the whole lot of us by midafternoon." Walid bent his head to the left, toward the path edged by wild bushes.

I wasn't about to give up that easily. "If we were careful . . . ."

"You don't know what careful means, to suggest something like that." He gestured to the paper in my hands. "To even make a list—don't you realize, this isn't a game?"

I stumbled over a tree root, then righted myself. "I'm not playing games," I said. If my voice sounded thick, well, perhaps I'd twisted my ankle. Or perhaps I was struggling with the feeling that Walid was treating me like a little girl. "I thought of all kinds of things we can do," I said. "This was just the first one. We could organize a protest, or send supplies across the border to the Iraqi fighters . . . ."

I stopped talking. The canopy and the clouds had combined to darken the sky; it felt more like dusk than early afternoon. Twilight, a time for lovers' meetings.

"You don't know much about me, do you?" asked Walid. He walked along the path sure-footedly, no stumbles for him. "Of course you don't. You want to know when I decided on this direction for my life? I didn't have to, you know. My family's well off; I scored high on my exams. I could have done anything. I did well in my chosen field in university. After graduation, I went to visit my uncle in Cairo."

We rounded the curve of the path, and the way in front of us lay clear. Stepping around a large boulder, Walid continued, "I was coming home from a bar—I'm not proud to say it, but I'm honest—with my arm around a girl I'd just met."

*Was she pretty?*

*Focus, Nadia, focus.*

"She wanted a pack of cigarettes, so we went into the nearby corner store. An old woman was in front of us, dressed in little more than rags. Her hands shook as she carried a can of olive oil to the counter. 'How much?' she asked. Either her eyesight was bad or she couldn't read, because the price, 12 pounds, was clearly marked on the side. 'Fifteen pounds,' said the shopkeeper. I remember thinking, that's not very Muslim of the shopkeeper. A good Muslim would give a poor woman a discount, not rip her off just because he had the chance."

Something brushed gently, like fingers, across my calves. What in the world? Oh. My cotton skirt, rustling in the unexpected breeze.

"Cheating a customer, inflicting hardship on an old woman, those things were much worse than drinking or having a girlfriend. Strangely, that only made me feel worse. Like it was all connected somehow. In school we read about Caliph Omar, and how under his rule, there was not one hungry person in the lands of Islam. I wished I lived in that society."

Still no one ahead and no one behind. Oh, I thought. He could take me in his arms now, cover me with kisses. Not that he would. Not that I should even be thinking about it. Not that I was thinking about it anymore. I was thinking about the relief at being alone with a boy and knowing you could trust him to behave properly.

"When I refused to buy cigarettes in the shop, the girl and I ended up arguing. She went her own way and I went home. There was no one in the apartment, but I didn't want to be alone, so I flicked on the television. The Israelis were persecuting the Palestinians, nothing new about that. I almost didn't pay attention. But there was one scene, a little girl, she couldn't have been more than six, outdoors in her nightclothes. She must have picked up a bomb or something, but I didn't see that. She was just standing there, her skin pale against her dark dress, staring at the place where her hand had been."

My mouth dropped open. "I remember that!" I said. But I didn't want to tell him that I'd cried for weeks, that even now, when I close my eyes, I can see that girl, her missing hand. "I remember that," I finished, not as loud the second time.

"I felt this incredible rage," he said. "I walked around the apartment, throwing things. Plates, glasses, vases, telephones— one by one they slammed against the wall, shattered, fell. The floor was sparkling with bits of colored glass, like a chandelier. The telephone came off the hook, *beep . . . beep . . . beep*. And then I realized something. I wasn't angry at Israel. I mean, of course, I was, but it was buried beneath a deeper, much more powerful rage. At myself, at all the Muslims."

The trees up ahead moved with the wind, almost as though nodding in agreement. "When did we become a society that lets its old people go hungry, lets its children die? When we accepted a foreign view of the way things should be."

I closed my eyes, just for a second. Sure enough, that little girl, big brown eyes bewildered, appeared with her mangled stump.

"Sorry," said Walid. "I didn't mean to go on like that." Too personal? We were walking such a thin Islamic line, an unmarried man and woman, plotting together. Avoid any hint of impropriety, keep the private behind strict, well-guarded lines. "I wanted you to know where I'm coming from. As I see it, we have three enemies: Muslims who are Muslims in name only, the ones who've left their religion behind and have accepted that the West rules the world; the Arab governments that bind us with their corruption and cruelty; and the West itself, which sets the agenda for a materialistic world that has nothing to do with Islam."

As he finished, the shelter of the trees broke and the scent of rain welcomed us back into the world. Ahead, the path opened into the wide meadow of the park. "In my opinion, whatever we do needs to affect all three targets. That's why the attacks on 9/11 were so successful. They shook up everybody; they changed the world."

That depended on how you defined success, didn't it? "Islam forbids the killing of innocent people just to make a point."

Walid stopped at the edge of the meadow. "The people in the World Trade Center were no more innocent than George Bush, Nadia."

"They weren't soldiers, they weren't government employees, they weren't—"

"They were people who benefited from the oppression of Muslims. They walk into their high-rise buildings in their thousand-dollar shoes because children in poor countries earn five cents per hour. People in the third world can't find jobs, can't get enough to eat, while Americans feast on exotic meat like alligator and—"

"My brother Nassir can't find a job and he goes to job fairs and posts his resume online, you don't see him killing anybody."

"Mustafa!"

Walid stood completely still at the sound of the unexpected voice. Not as disciplined, I looked around. The young man in a green windbreaker seemed to appear out of nowhere. He waved wildly at Walid, and began to run in our direction. Waiting a heartbeat, until the young man came close enough to hear, Walid said, "You're not lost, miss. If you walk across the meadow and out through the gate, you'll find Sharia al-Nile right there. You can catch a bus to Midan easily." He turned to the young man and put an arm around him. "Dear friend," he said. They exchanged kisses on both cheeks.

"Mustafa," said Dear Friend. "The last place I expected to find you is the park." He didn't glance in my direction. There was nothing to do but walk away.

My natural canopy gone, I was back in the real world with a vengeance. I looked at my watch. 2:00. The real world, where I had to cross an hour of city in twenty minutes. Where unexpected rain clouds gathered angrily in the sky, ready to pour buckets on my head. Where once again—how could I have been so stupid?—I'd left Walid without any plans to meet. Right in the midst of an argument that belied my commitment to saving the Muslims. An argument that proved to him, probably, that I was still a frightened little girl. I might well never hear from him again.

Who needs rain? Tears swam in front of my eyes. I longed to think of something coded and mysterious that I could say to arrange a rendezvous under the nose of Dear Friend, whoever he was. Chum from Walid's old life? Someone who worked with him, had gone to school with him? Even—I shivered—secret police? I couldn't think of anything clever enough. And if I could have, I wouldn't have dared.

I didn't even dare to turn around, to watch the place where he had been. Instead, I followed the path he sent me on, across the meadow and around to the gate. Out of the park and out of my ten-second experiment as a holy warrior.

# In the Name of God, the Bestower, the One Who Gives Plenty Without Return

By the time I got off the bus, raindrops had started falling. I'd almost reached the bottom of our steps before the clouds opened and the rain poured out.

When I pushed open the front door, the rooms inside were dark. And silent. I checked my watch. 2:37. Not bad, since everything slows down during the rain. So why was all quiet on the home front? My heart sped up a bit, pounding out that faster rhythm I was getting used to. Was there any way my mother could have found out I left school early? Had Miss called to make sure I'd arrived home safely?

I bit my lip. "Mama?" No answer. I made my way to the living room. "Mama?" The lights were off in the salon; the darkening sky outside lent the room an ominous feel. It wasn't until I almost tripped over him that I saw Nassir.

"What's the matter with you? You had to hear me calling."

"Don't get in such a panic. Mama went over to Auntie Um Bassam's. Afternoon of tea and gossip, maybe make a few dress patterns."

I stared at him as best I could in the dim light. There was something unusual about Nassir today, some surprising quality. What was it? "She didn't tell me she was going there."

"Does she have to tell you everything?"

I tossed my book bag onto the coffee table and threw myself into a chair. "Why do you sound so happy anyway?" That was the difference: Nassir was smiling. "Is someone engaged? Is it you? Is that why you're sitting here in the dark, dreaming of the night you carry your bride off to some fancy hotel on the Mediterranean coast?"

"Typical woman, all you think about is marriage."

I picked up my book bag and raised it over my head, ready to throw it at him. "You don't have the courage," said Nassir. "And you couldn't hit the side of a billboard with a moving truck."

I threw. The bag clunked against his knees. "Ow," he said. "Fine, I surrender. I wasn't going to say anything until I was sure—don't breathe a word to Mama—but I think I've got a job."

I wanted to say "Congratulations!" and throw confetti in the air. Part of me did, anyway. The other part got in first. "How'd you get it? Mahmoud?"

"Nope. Bassam."

Bassam to the rescue. Again. "Bassam? Whom does he know?"

"Some friend of his in the Emirates, who knew someone here who knew someone else . . . . I had my first interview today—and you know what? I think it went well. The boss, he's a young guy, he liked me, I could tell."

I bent my legs, pulled my feet up on the couch, and rested my chin on my knees. "Well, congratulations," I said. No confetti, no brass band, but my spirits had lifted. "Mama has no idea? Did you tell Mohammad?—Hey, where are Sarah and the girls, anyway?"

He frowned. "In case you hadn't noticed, they've been at her mother's for the last five days. And Mama won't let me take my room back because she insists it's only normal that Sarah spend time with her family, and she'll return soon enough."

"Well, maybe she and the girls will learn some religion there. Mama's much too lenient with them—"

The door opened then and Mama came in, dripping wet and carrying a plastic bag filled with greens. I bit my lip. She hates it when I complain about Sarah. *A Muslimah should be generous in spirit.*

She hadn't heard me, or else she'd decided to be generous herself. "Nadia, come and take these, please," she said, pulling the scarf off her head and shrugging out of her drenched coat. "Who would have expected it to rain today? And why are you two sitting in the dark? Nassir, did you close all the windows?"

"We're in the dark because the electricity went out," said Nassir. "Been out since one o'clock."

Mama paused, her arm suspended in midair with the bag of greens. "It wasn't the rain, then?"

"No idea," said Nassir.

I took the greens, dripping with water like Mama, and walked into the kitchen. Through the window I could see buckets of rain stampeding on the grass below. Ridiculous, but I felt a little stab of fear. Didn't the lights go out in Baghdad just before the Americans invaded? Hadn't Bush been threatening Syria for months—stop supporting terrorists, stop funding insurgents, and other accusations he couldn't prove? Suppose it was our turn to have our city sacked, pious people thrown into prison, foreign boots patrolling our streets?

"Nadia?" Mama came into the kitchen, her wet clothes swapped for a cotton housedress. "Why are you just standing there? You're getting water all over the floor."

"Sorry." I moved across to the kitchen and dropped the wet bag in the sink. "Chop the parsley, please—we'll have *tabouli* salad for dinner and there should be some of the leftover potatoes from yesterday." She opened the refrigerator and began shifting the contents inside. "How was school today?"

She spoke in a normal voice, a casual voice. Trying to restore our easygoing relationship? I wanted to respond in kind, but I couldn't help remembering that I'd skipped school today, I'd met a strange boy in the park, I'd wandered beneath the trees with him. Was there a trap hidden underneath her innocent question? "Fine," I said, as clipped as I could. I didn't dare risk more than that.

After dinner, after cleanup, we still had no power. I sat at the tiny desk in the corner of my bedroom, a thin candle lighting up the first column of my math book. A knock sounded against the door, and Nassir came in.

"Sorry to disturb you," he said. "Just on my way to the balcony. Mama went downstairs to complain about the blackout with Auntie Um Suheil—not much for me to do in a dark and empty house."

I sighed and pushed back my chair. "I can't get any work done anyway," I said. "Nassir, you don't think something terrible is about to happen, do you? That they've cut our power on purpose, so we don't have any contact with the outside world?"

"Don't be ridiculous." He'd dropped his usual sneering tone, though. "Syria's a third world country, that's all. Things don't always work the way they're supposed to." He propped himself up against Mama's bureau. "That's all," he said again.

"I think it's what happened that makes me worry so much. What happened to Fowzi, I mean. It's been weeks, I know, but I'm still, I'm not myself."

I never talked about Fowzi. Never. There was a long silence before Nassir said, "What happened to Fowzi changed all of us. Like Samira wearing *hijab*. I don't think anybody can go on the way they were before. I know I can't."

Nassir's words touched me. I'd no idea he felt so strongly about Fowzi's arrest. Hoping to hide the catch in my voice, I said, "Well, except Yasmine."

"That's not fair." Nassir's sneer was back. "Not true, either."

I drummed my pencil against the top of the desk. "You mean her new classes?"

Nassir shifted his weight against the bureau. "Yasmine has given up something very important to her, important but destructive. It was incredibly difficult for her to, ah, get herself out of this situation, but she did it. And she did it because of how much it would horrify Fowzi if he knew. So don't say she hasn't changed."

Nassir wasn't looking at me. In the dim candlelight, I probably couldn't have seen his expression if he were. "You're talking about that boy from Mezzah."

Nassir's head flew up. "What do you know about that?"

"Nothing," I said. "Just what Auntie Um Suheil repeated."

"Nasty old gossip."

At least she doesn't eavesdrop at doors. My face grew hot and I turned back to my book. A minute later, Nassir continued on his way to the balcony. I sat at my desk until the candle burned down, but didn't turn another page.

In the Name of God,
the Guide,
He Who Guides Whom He Wills

No one wanted to go on a picnic.

It was too easy to remember that the last picnic we all shared included Fowzi. Too easy for me, at least. And the long silence that followed Bassam's suggestion indicated that I wasn't the only one remembering.

"Well, then, I have another idea," he said, standing up and stepping over the row of feet—mine, Nassir's, Yasmine's, and Samira's—that lined up below the couch in our salon. "We all look like we could use some fun—let me make a phone call or two."

Friday. Plenty of time for the city to have recovered from its blackout—we woke up the next morning with lights blazing through the house—and plenty of time for me to recover from my fears. But between lessons and cups of tea and chores, I hadn't come up with any new ideas for sniffing out Walid.

Helpless, and all my own fault. I could always resort to a message via the old beggar on the corner. Did he still beg on that corner, though? I couldn't remember the last time I'd seen him there. And that look on his face as I'd walked away . . . . He wasn't one of them—one of *us*—he was frightened. Was it fair to drag a broke and broken man in deeper still?

Scratch the beggar, then. Did I have any other options? Yarmuk. That's where I'd first noticed Walid, and it was just the sort of chaotic, underworld kind of place where a revolution could thrive. Was I brave enough to trek out there alone, though? And was I smart enough to drum up a clever excuse to stay home?

Auntie Um Noah could always use company. We hadn't visited her for weeks—then again, would anyone believe that I'd go there without being prodded? A more acceptable option: say I'd stay to do the weekend housekeeping, give Mama a break.

"Good news," said Bassam, hanging up the phone. "I've borrowed a car and we'll go to Zabadani for the afternoon."

Only a half-hour drive from Damascus, Zabadani straddles the Lebanese border. High in the mountains, snow lasts until spring. No snow now, of course, but the temperature would be at least ten degrees cooler than the heat wave that had oppressed the city after the freak rainstorm. Add in spectacular views, the treats Bassam was sure to buy everyone . . . .

"I'll stay home, do all the cleaning, give Mama a break," said Nassir. He caught my eye and bent his head in the direction of the just-abandoned telephone. There was always the off-chance that his prospective employer might call. "How long has it been since you went to Zabadani, Mama?"

"Oh," said Mama. She waved her hands in a halfhearted protest. "I promised Auntie Um Fowzi I'd spend the afternoon with her. You know she doesn't like to sit alone. And the housekeeping won't take that long."

"Yes, it will," said Nassir, a new firmness in his voice. "You go out to Harasta, and Bassam will take the girls to Zabadani."

An hour later, I found myself perched between my cousins at a tiny table on the edge of the mountaintop, the breeze ruffling my scarf. The breathtaking views—slopes of green grasses, pockets of waving flowers, cottages dotted here and there along the winding roads—didn't disappoint. In front of me sat a half-drunk Pepsi and a platter of assorted pastries.

Yasmine babbled on about her first English class. "Not one word of Arabic. If anyone slips up, the professor says 'I don'unnerstan.' By the end of the year, we'll all be fluent, or nearly."

"English is useful," said Samira. "But it's so ugly. If I go to Geneva, I'll need to learn French." She giggled and looked at her sister. "The language of love."

"I agree that English and French are useful," I said. It was the first comment I'd made since we sat down. "But I hate the idea of using the colonial language. Arabic is a worldwide language—why doesn't anyone from the West ever learn it?"

Bassam chose the largest piece of *bakhlava*. "English isn't a colonial language anymore, Nadia," he said. He took a bite of honey-drenched pastry. "People from Japan use it to communicate with people from Saudi Arabia. It's a global language now."

"It's still their language, and they make money from exporting it, and make money because they speak it well. Everything with them is about money." I didn't mean to sound so bitter. After all, I was luckier than most girls in Damascus, many of whom had never even seen Zabadani.

"That's not true," said Bassam through another mouthful of *bakhlava*. "Americans are the same as you or me, Nadia—they want what's best for their families, they want peace and prosperity."

"Then they're not like me." The scent of jasmine blew in on the fresh breeze. "I want to follow God's commands and be a good *Muslimah*. Anyway, you're just saying that because your visa's about to come through and you're going to live there. Which I still don't see how you can do."

Yasmine reached for a piece of *bakhlava*, then drew back her hand. "You'd never move there, not for any reason, Nadia? Not even to complete your training as a doctor?"

I blew air out over my bottom lip, reaching for the same effect as the breeze but failing. "I used to think I could," I said. "But now—I'm so angry with them. They live their expensive lives, with their high-rise buildings and thousand-dollar shoes, and they never bother to ask the question: why do people hate us? Never think that, to the rest of the world, they're rich because we're poor." I blew air out again, this time just to take a breath.

Fine, the high rise, the thousand-dollar shoes, those lines

came straight from Walid. But the rest of it, that was pure Nadia. Things I'd been thinking about for a long time but had never had the words or the courage to say.

"That's more the argument of the communist party," Bassam said. He spoke easily but I sensed an undercurrent of something in his voice. "U.S. consumption and production create markets, Nadia, they don't exploit them. The whole world is better off now than a thousand years ago, or fifty, because Americans make and distribute products that benefit us all."

"Here, here," said Samira, banging her soda bottle down on the table. "What would I do without my Pepsi?"

I ignored her. "Can you deny that the people killed in 9/11 were able to buy their computers and TVs and fancy cars because children in the third world earn five cents an hour?"

"I just did," said Bassam. He gestured to the waiter and ordered another round of Pepsis.

We sat in almost silence, because I didn't count Yasmine's chatter about the boy in her class who'd gone to English school in the Gulf and taught all the other boys vulgar words. Innocents, that's the point Bassam was trying to make, the same thing I'd said to Walid. But was it enough not to be involved? It wasn't enough for a Muslim. "Command the good, forbid the evil," said the Prophet. Words to live by. There was a Western phrase that argued the same thing. What was it? Oh, yes: *All that's necessary for evil to triumph is for good men to do nothing.* Didn't that mean that the do-nothings weren't good people anymore?

But did it mean they deserved to die?

I couldn't quite wrap my head around that idea. Instead, I floated back into the conversation. "Just wait till the boys see how much better the girls do on exams," Samira was saying. She flashed a look at me. "Women didn't have to blow up buildings or behead people to earn the right to vote. They just proved their equality by excelling in all fields."

The second round of drinks arrived. "I thought I knew you all so well," said Bassam. "But you continue to surprise me."

He meant me. I shrugged and took a cheese pastry. What was the point in saying anything? They were never going to agree with me.

I rode home in the backseat beside Samira, who twisted the ends of her scarf and let it pull free in the wind. "Do you want to come in?" I asked when Bassam stopped in the parking lot beside our building.

"You know, I think I'll pass," he said. "It's late and I've got to get the car back. But if you girls want to . . . ."

"No," said Yasmine. "It'll be such a bother to get a taxi later." They sent their *salaams* to Mama and Nassir. I waited till the car had pulled away and the lights faded in the distance. It was much too late to head out to Yarmuk, but I could at least check the corner and see if the lame beggar was propped against his usual traffic light. Maybe, just maybe, Walid was sitting in for him again. I hadn't put much space between me and the garden when I heard a familiar voice. "Nadia," called Auntie Um Suheil. "Is that you? I know it's late, but there's something important we need to talk about."

Important? Auntie Um Suheil? I doubted it. Still, seventeen years of respect for my elders prevailed, and I headed to her apartment.

# In the Name of God,
## the Manifest

"Good evening," said Auntie Um Suheil. Her large frame filled the doorway. She bent over to kiss me on each cheek and I smelled the remnants of her dinner, garlic and onion and cumin. "Come in and have some tea."

I tried to hide my resentment. No time to sneak out to Yarmuk, no time to sort out my feelings about terrorism, but I was supposed to find time for Auntie Um Suheil and her gossip? "Thank you, Auntie, you're too kind, but I've been out all day and I need to get my lessons done."

She pulled me inside and closed the door. "You have time for a cup of tea," she said. "You young girls, it's all lessons, lessons, all the time. No time to be polite. When I was a girl, things were different."

Wishing I had the courage to walk out the door, I followed Auntie Um Suheil into the small kitchen she shared with her sister-in-law. Dishes from dinner elbowed each other along the laminated counter, one and all covered with expensive aluminum foil. She moved one aside to make room for a kettle of water and a tiny tray just big enough for two teacups.

I couldn't stop thinking about what Bassam had said long enough to pay attention to Auntie's chatter. All that nonsense about America making the world a better place. A place filled with AK-47s, sniper fire, and violent prisons, that's what they'd made.

*Don't think about fingernail pliers and electric wires and rubber hoses and Tadmor Prison and Fowzi and lack of sunlight and no water and—don't think about it.*

PAULA JOLIN

I opened my eyes. Auntie Um Suheil stood beside the counter, a spoonful of sugar balanced on the edge of a teacup, looking at me expectantly. "One," I said. "I take one spoon."

"That's right." She prattled on, and I lost the thread of the conversation after the third word. Maybe betraying Fowzi was more than a visa to Bassam. Maybe he'd bought the party line: suppress them into prosperity. Round up supposed terrorists, plunk them in prisons—kill them before they commit violence.

"So, what are you going to do?" Auntie Um Suheil placed the tiny tray on the table in front of me. I stared. "About Sarah," she said. "Don't pretend you haven't thought about it, Nadia. A man needs to know his wife will stick by him no matter what, and not go rushing home to her mother. People are starting to talk."

I continued to stare. If anyone was talking, it was Auntie Um Suheil.

"That's between her and Mohammad," I said at last. I took a sip of tea. "I can't do anything about it, anyway."

"*Divorce* is an ugly word," said Auntie Um Suheil. "An ugly thing to have in the family." She looked at me meaningfully. I looked back. Maybe in rural Syria thirty years ago, a girl with a divorced sister-in-law couldn't get married herself, but in modern Damascus, boys don't care about things like that. "Of all the permitted things, divorce is the most hated by God," she added.

Why not let it go, keep my mouth shut, finish my tea? That's what I should have done. Instead, I said, "Divorce isn't always a bad thing, you know."

Auntie Um Suheil goggled at me.

I didn't care. "Look at the way those girls are growing up. Sarah watches TV all day and paints her nails, never a thought in her head about God." My resentment of decadent Muslims was spilling over, but I couldn't seem to stop myself. "She's no better than an Unbeliever. Not much better. If they divorced, Mama could take custody of the girls, and then Sarah could marry someone else, someone Westernized and rich."

I took a sip of tea, still so hot it burned my tongue.

"Sarah's not as advanced in religion as you are, Nadia." Auntie Um Suheil lifted her own cup of tea and blew across the top.

I clicked my burned tongue. "I'm not advanced. But when it says in the Qur'an 'put a scarf on your head,' I put it on. When it says 'pray,' I get down on my knees. It's not that hard to figure out."

She blew again. "I don't know what's come over you, Nadia."

What had come over me? Maybe an understanding that God rewards the Believers who follow His laws.

What would it take to force the infidels to flee the ruthless desert sun? More Muslims following God's law, that was certain. Every step backward the Unbelievers had taken, however small, has been the result of pious men standing up for justice. Believers strapped bombs around their waists to blow up buses and enemies, and bingo—the world was calling for an end to illegal occupation.

Insurgents or patriots? Terrorists—my mind quailed at the word—or good men who refuse to watch evil and do nothing? Rebels or the Founding Fathers of our future Islamic Empire?

I drained my teacup and set it on the table. "I'm the same girl I've always been, Auntie," I said. "I'm just braver now." Pushing back the metal chair, I stood up.

She frowned. "All this wasn't what I called you for, Nadia."

I paused, my hand on the doorknob.

Auntie Um Suheil turned back to the counter and shifted a few more dishes. She fished out an envelope smeared with an unappetizing stain. "Here," she said, offering it to me. "I found it this afternoon tucked under the mat—it probably came with the mail yesterday, but I must have missed it."

*To the Haddad family* had been scrawled across the front. I turned the envelope over. *P.O. Box 2289710 Damascus* I read. That wasn't what caught my interest though. Right above it, in tiny print, someone had penciled in the words *In God We Trust.* In English.

My heart beat faster. "Thanks," I said. "And thanks for the tea." I managed to stay under control until I'd climbed the first set of stairs and crossed the landing. Then I ripped the envelope open. Inside, nothing but a yellow receipt. Four bunches of flowers at 250 lira each; that came to 1,000 lira. I frowned, until I reached the bottom line. *Delivery info*, someone had added in a strong hand. *1500 Sharia Salah al-Din. Across the street from the National War Museum. Tuesday.*

# In the Name of God,
## the Unique,
## the One Without a Partner

I saw him even before I climbed off the bus. Dressed in khaki pants and a white button-down shirt, he leaned against the edge of the ticket booth. A briefcase rested at his feet. Was this his real identity, harried young professional, or just another disguise?

He checked his watch just before I crossed the road, and then again when I reached midpoint. Part of the props, or was he impatient to see me? A car barreled down the road and, heart racing, I scurried the last few feet to join him.

"*Salaam aleikum*, Nadia."

"*Aleikum salaam*." At least I didn't sound as breathless as I felt.

He leaned into the window of the booth and paid both our admission fees. I had never been to the war museum before but at least no one I knew would be there. As a pleasant surprise, it was beautiful: guns and tanks and ammunition housed amid the ruins of an ancient palace. We entered the courtyard, walked across smooth black and white tiles, stared at the walls decorated with intricate patterns of colorful calligraphy.

An old man in rumpled pants and a skullcap approached us and offered a guided tour. Walid pressed a few notes into his palm and waved him away.

"You know, we should organize some way of communicating," I said at last, when it seemed like Walid would never speak. "I could give you my phone number, as long as you promise to hang up if anyone else answers. My mother and brothers would have a

PAULA JOLIN

fit if some strange boy rang up and wanted to speak to me."

Walid looked amused. "Why do you think I haven't called you?" We stopped in front of the first of many rooms leading off the courtyard. "I have your number—Fowzi gave it to me once, in case I had to contact him there."

Oh. I waited, but he didn't offer his own number. It took a minute to get up the courage to say, "Maybe we could arrange someplace to leave messages, then? Suppose Auntie had given the envelope to my mother or my brother Nassir instead of me?"

Walid switched his briefcase from one hand to the other. "It wouldn't have meant anything to them."

"They would have crumpled it up and thrown it away. I'd have missed the rendezvous."

We looked into the first room, stocked with examples of the rifles that rebel Syrians had used against the French during occupation. "Don't you think if you didn't come today, I'd arrange another meeting?"

My face flushed and I stared at the ground. Half of what I wanted: a promise that we'd meet again. No way to contact him myself, though. What if there was an emergency? I curbed my impatience and said instead, "I thought you were mad at me, maybe, because of what I said last time. About 9/11."

We had the museum almost to ourselves. The ticket taker was out of sight, and the guide had retreated to a patch of shade in the far corner. Perfect scenario: private enough to say what we wanted, no dangerous opportunities to be alone. "I wasn't mad at you. Just surprised. From what Fowzi said, I thought you saw the world as it really is, not as you'd like it to be."

"I don't think I'm looking at the world all wrong," I told him as we moved to the next room, which was studded with pieces of shrapnel and grenades. "I'm not as sure as you are that violence is the only answer."

Funny how sure I seemed to be when I was with people from the other side. Then again, what was at stake, arguing with

Samira and Bassam? Loud voices, brutal arguments, maybe a hurt feeling or two.

He switched his briefcase again, and the edge of his sleeve brushed the lower part of my arm. Cloth against cloth, but still I flinched. "Yes, but they're the ones who set the agenda for violence, Nadia," he said in a low voice. "They don't pay attention to anything else, not UN resolutions, not civil disobedience. George Bush called tens of millions of people protesting around the world a focus group."

Had George Bush really said that?

"Look at Palestine. A peaceful boycott in effect for ten years—does anyone pay attention to it? It's only when people start getting killed that the world takes note."

I stared up at him. He looked less athletic and virile in this incarnation than he had as a teenage soccer star, but I found him more intriguing: older, sure of what he wanted, a man. The smell of sweat and ground dirt that clung to him during our last encounter had been replaced by the faintest hint of exotic cologne. Had the Prophet forbidden men to wear scent? I'd heard that somewhere, but I must have heard wrong.

*You're having a discussion, Nadia. Discuss.* "So, you're saying we should let them set the agenda?"

He leaned the briefcase against the courtyard wall and took a handkerchief out of his pocket. For the first time I noticed the sun, hot and full on the back of my covered neck. "They don't want democracy, Nadia. Look at Algeria, look at Iran—when a Muslim country holds a free election and elects religious leaders, the West cries foul." He looked around, lowered his voice. "Who supported Saddam Hussein? Who supports Mubarak, the House of Saud? They don't want the Middle East governed by the will of the people, they want it governed by sleazy politicians who stick to a Western agenda."

I wished I had thought to bring a handkerchief of my own.

"Look, Nadia, if you're not sure about this, no one says you have to be involved. You could be helpful, I admit that. But not if I have to come see you every day for a year to get you to agree."

I didn't answer.

"Not everyone is cut out for this," he added. "Some people are more suited to sit on the sidelines than to change the world. That doesn't have to be a bad thing. Look at all the Meccans who only became Muslim after the Prophet conquered the city. They're still admired and looked up to, though they didn't have the sense or the courage to listen when they heard the message the first time."

I didn't admire the Meccans who'd fought against the Prophet's crusade until it proved to their advantage to join. Was there any greater insult than being called a me-too Muslim?

We were no longer alone in the museum. Two foreign women came in, both young, university students probably. They were laughing and speaking English. "And then what did he say?"

"He said he didn't mean to bother me, he just wanted to marry me. Some stranger on the street—these people are outrageous."

"Well, it's nice to know they don't all hate us," said the other woman, tugging at the bottom of her shirt. "And at least tomorrow we'll be going to the seashore. Abdul says the people there are much more tolerant, and we can wear shorts, and swim." They moved into the room with the rifles, out of earshot.

"Iran has the right idea," said Walid. "Make all foreign women wear *hijab*." Both girls wore jeans, the kind that hug tight at the waist and hips and let loose at the bottom. One had on a bright red shirt, short sleeves, with gold sparkles. The other had a white shirt with no sleeves at all. They were both blond, with earrings and makeup, sunglasses balanced on the tops of their heads, and they had those thin, curveless bodies so prized in the West.

Was that the kind of body Walid found attractive? Another reason to wear a *manteau*. My body dips and bulges in unexpected places, without the clear, smooth lines of the girls on the other side of the museum. I was glad Walid couldn't see it.

"Ignorant girls," he added.

Ignorant, yes, of God's goodness and greatness and commands. But did they deserve to die for it?

I didn't know I'd spoken my thoughts out loud until Walid answered me. "This isn't about innocent or guilty. If those girls died in a violent explosion, yes, it would be sad. But any sadder than the Palestinian girls, the same age, who've died when Israeli commanders firebombed their house? Any sadder than the Iraqi girls caught in American sniper fire? You need to pick sides, Nadia—wasn't it George Bush who said, 'You're for us or against us?'"

It was that stark, wasn't it? If we acted, foreigners might die. If we didn't, Muslims would.

I thought of Shaykh AbdulHalim annihilated by Israeli bombs; Nassir and Mohammad, sinking in misery as the Western exploitation of the third world left them without jobs; the Palestinian girl whose missing hand had haunted me for years. Fowzi, dragged from his apartment, bruised and bleeding.

Walid picked up his briefcase. Was this it—did it contain a bomb he was about to lob at the foreign interlopers? *The things you think, Nadia.* He turned and crossed the courtyard, descended down the back steps. I followed him, scrambling through a small garden blooming with pink and white flowers, climbing a short flight of stone steps behind him.

I caught him at the top, the former *madrasa* where students lived hundreds of years ago, now transformed into an international craft fair. I managed to stop myself from reaching out and touching his hand. "I'm a Muslim," I said. "That's all the answer you need."

Walid turned to the first booth, where mother-of-pearl boxes, chess sets, and tiny inlaid tables covered every available surface. Despite the heat of the day, I shivered. "In that case," he said, "I'll be in touch."

The middle-aged proprietor didn't look up as I examined a set of small, intricately pieced boxes, and when I turned one over, I knew why. The price tag screamed *For Tourists Only!* I placed it back on the table and took a deep breath. *Tomorrow, 2 p.m.* That way I can tell Mama I have to stay after school for extra help with Miss. I turned my head to suggest the time to Walid. What Walid? He was gone.

I spun around. At the end of the row of booths, I saw a flash of khaki disappear around the corner. Who needs dignity? I hoisted my purse over my shoulder and took off after him. Behind me, the shopkeeper called out, probably thinking my swift exit meant I had stolen something. Let him prove it.

I darted in and out of milling customers, overheard a few snickers—"It's a hot day to run, isn't it, pretty girl?"—and sent a toddler almost sprawling. His outraged scream and his mother's angry comments reached my ears as I slowed my pace and turned the corner. I walked quickly around the side of the booths. To my right, the road headed up into town; to my left, cars sped down the highway that led out to Mezzah. I looked in both directions. No Walid up, no Walid down.

Or—who was that? Pulling himself aboard the back entrance to a full-length bus?

I ran again.

# In the Name of God,
## the Abaser,
## the One Who Lowers Whom He Wills

I slid twice on the rocky sidewalk as I made my way up the steep road. Walid had disappeared into the crush of male bodies crammed in the center aisle, hanging on to metal poles or ceiling straps. Probably upright, straight, glancing at his watch, looking like any other impatient businessman.

The lights on the back of the bus flickered once and then again, as though the driver was getting ready to pull into traffic. I sprinted. A burst of energy, over the curb, snaking past the careening cars— and with a roar, the bus jerked forward and into the road.

I grimaced. Now I'd have to wait for Walid to contact me. At least he'd said he would, he'd promised, not once but twice. Still, I wasn't happy about it. I carried a heavy feeling with me through the long walk back to school, the lesson on electromagnetic properties, the final bell that sent us all home. Still lethargic, I tiptoed past Auntie Um Suheil's front door—I couldn't take talking to her, not today—and came up the steps.

I pushed the door open. ". . . defend your behavior," Mohammad was saying. "Do you think I don't know that you're rude to my mother, to my sister?"

"And your sister isn't rude to me? With all her 'Here's my prayer mat, Sarah, if you want to use it,' and 'Do you want me to teach Mariam and Dimah how to pray?' Like I'm some kind of infidel. All her '*hijab* makes me feel so free' comments. You're raising a little extremist, do you know that? The next thing that happens she'll be off in Iraq, waving hand grenades at the Americans."

I placed one hand on the doorjamb. What to do now? Sneak back down the stairs and suffer through Auntie Um Suheil's afternoon tea? Take a walk around the block? Of course, I did neither. "This isn't about my sister," said Mohammad. "This is about the fact that you're my wife, and I have some say over your behavior, and over where you live. You're obligated to live with me—remember? We signed a marriage contract."

Sandals shuffled across the floor. "A marriage contract that gave me rights, too," Sarah said. "The right to a proper house, with my own kitchen, and my own rooms. Like we had in the Emirates. Do you think I like coming back to this backwater country with the left-behind fashions, where everyone sits around discussing sewing patterns and stories of the Prophet?"

"I refuse to talk about that now."

Shuffle, shuffle. "I'm not living here, that's it. Either you find me a decent place to live, a home of my own, in a respectable part of town—I'm not living out in Harasta—or I'm staying with my mother. The girls, too."

"Sarah, I have to insist you move back here. Otherwise—"

"Divorce me then," said Sarah.

At that moment, a hand squeezed my shoulder. I shrieked. Mama had come up the steps, a shopping bag filled with something green, and behind her bobbed the heads of Yasmine and Samira. Yasmine's arms were filled with fruit and vegetables, but Samira had her school bag slung over her shoulder. I hadn't noticed them, hadn't heard their steps or the rustle of their bags, hadn't smelled the drench of Yasmine's perfume, hadn't seen . . . anything.

"Who's that?" asked Mohammad, covering the distance to the door before he finished the question. Sarah was right behind him. "Your sister," said Sarah. Her tone of voice added: See? I told you you had no idea what your sister would do.

"Were you all standing here listening to us?" Mohammad's face darkened.

"Listening to what?" asked Mama. "We just got here. Yasmine and I went to the vegetable stand, and Samira found us there when she got off the bus, and then we ran into Nadia. At the bottom of the stairs," she added. I directed my gaze to the ground. I couldn't bear to see the look on Samira's face, or catch her exchanging glances with her sister. "I was trying to get her to carry the bag for me, but she wouldn't."

"Why did she scream then?" asked Sarah.

"I pinched her. What kind of girl won't help her mother up the stairs?" Mama handed a slack-wristed Mohammad the bag. "Could you take this please? Or do you refuse to help your mother too?"

Mohammad took the bag and looked in it.

"Is something wrong?" asked Mama. "Were you two fighting?"

Sarah and Mohammad didn't look at each other, and for a moment they didn't say anything, either. Then, "No," said Sarah. "Of course we weren't fighting. I just don't like to be spied on." She still didn't look at Mohammad, but she looked hard and cold and straight at me.

In the Name of God,
the Subtle One,
the Gracious


Mama and my cousins burst into speech at the same time, trying to drown out the echo of Sarah's unkind comment. Yasmine was saying, "You know, I've lost almost four kilos" as she left her bags on the kitchen counter and followed her sister into the salon. Before I could tag along, Mama said quietly, "Nadia, I want to talk to you a minute, please."

I watched Sarah disappear into her bedroom, Mohammad escape in the direction of the balcony, Yasmine and Samira settle themselves on the couch in the salon. Then I joined Mama in the kitchen.

I expected her to ask me to chop or grind or slice something, but she sat at the kitchen table, chin resting in the palms of her hands.

"What's for dinner?" I asked.

For a long minute, there was nothing to hear but Samira and Yasmine's muted laughter in the salon and the buzzing of mosquitoes as they butted their heads against the window. Then Mama said, "What was the meaning of all that nonsense about Sarah?"

"I didn't want to listen." I could only imagine what she had thought, finding me skulking in the doorway. "At first, I meant to come in, but it seemed so awkward, and then, well, they were talking about me. I couldn't seem to walk away."

I waited for the chastisement: proper Muslims don't listen at keyholes. But Mama stared at me a long time before she said, "No, I mean telling Auntie Um Suheil that Sarah's not a practicing Muslim, that she's the next thing to an Unbeliever. Do you know Auntie Um Suheil came here and asked me if Sarah is having an affair? If she asked me, she's going to be telling everybody else."

Worse than eavesdropping. "I didn't say anything like that." Even to my own ears the words sounded feeble. "I said that Dimah and Mariam would be better off brought up by people who pray. That's it. Anything else, it's coming straight out of Auntie Um Suheil's imagination."

"Do you have any idea of how devastating this kind of rumor could be to Sarah, to those girls?"

I did. How to explain to Mama, though, how much it hurt me that everyone in my family seemed to be drifting away from Islam? How much I wanted Sarah, Yasmine, Samira to pray, to love God, to lead proper Muslim lives? Even Bassam—I couldn't bear him disappearing into the moral mess of America.

How to say all that without sounding like a fanatic of the worst sort?

I leaned on the refrigerator, letting its vibrations throb against my back. "It's not my fault some gossipmonger is spreading rumors when she should be reading Qur'an."

*Why weren't you reading Qur'an instead of telling tales about Sarah?* I knew I needed to apologize, not defend myself, but somehow I couldn't. I'm as fallible as the next person, struggling to walk the straight path. Why does it seem to me that everyone else is going about it the wrong way?

Mama sighed.

A knock sounded on the front door. As the silence stretched between us, the knocking went unanswered. At last Yasmine called out, "I'll get it, Auntie." From my position inside the kitchen, I saw her fly to the door, swing it open, and let Bassam inside. "Auntie, do you need help in the kitchen?" she asked. When Mama said no, a beaming Yasmine escorted Bassam to the salon.

Mama rested her hands on the table. "The years of tempta-tion, everyone told me to watch out for them. I thought they meant boys, short skirts, falling in love with someone unsuitable. All those things I was prepared for. But this . . . ."

"Shouldn't we be starting dinner?" I interrupted. Mama was more accurate than she knew. Secret meetings with a boy, impure thoughts, chasing after buses.

Maybe I was truly angry because I was the one unable to lead an Islamic life.

If only the stupid Americans weren't out proclaiming their message against so-called terrorism and ruining all our lives. If only the stupid government had left Fowzi alone. That's when all this started, wasn't it? When I realized that it was up to me to do something about the screwed-up world we live in?

Mama didn't answer my question about dinner. Instead, she said, "Nadia, where do you think all this extremist rhetoric is going to get you? To prison, like your cousin."

I pressed my lips together. "I don't want to talk about Fowzi."

"That's the problem," said Mama. "By refusing to talk about him, you're imagining all kinds of crazy scenarios—none of which is likely to be true."

I pushed away from the refrigerator door. My voice was rising, but I couldn't seem to stop it. "How do you know what's true? How does anybody? We live in a world of secrecy and rumor, a world where we have no control over anything."

"Nadia, please."

"Please what?" I moved back toward the hallway. "Keep my voice down about the government? Stop criticizing the stupid Americans for bashing around the world blindfolded?"

"You can't blame everything on the Americans, Nadia."

I had reached the hall. In the salon, Samira, Yasmine, and Bassam had given up pretending conversation and goggled at me. I didn't care. "You know as well as I do that Fowzi was arrested because the Americans pressured the Syrian government to 'crack down on terrorism or feel our wrath.' He's probably in their hands right now, part of a naked pyramid, or dead on the cement floor of a cell somewhere."

I turned and fled down the hall. Someone sobbed—Yasmine. As I rushed through the salon, I saw Bassam turn and put a soothing arm around her shoulder. I couldn't stand the fact that I had nowhere to go, nowhere to be alone. Rushing down the short corridor, I bolted into the bathroom and slammed the door.

Then I turned the lock.

In the Name of God,
the Self-Sufficient

I stayed in the bathroom a long time. Mama cajoled, Samira begged, Mohammad pounded on the door. Mariam came out of her mother's bedroom and threatened to pee on the floor.

After what seemed like hours, they abandoned me and sat down to eat. The clink of silverware, the swish of bread mopping up sauce, and the sound of subdued conversation carried them through dinner. Not long after, the clash of plates rang out as the girls carried dirty dishes to the kitchen. From a distance, I heard my cousins saying good-bye. I took the opportunity to escape into our empty bedroom and hide under the covers.

"You're behaving like a child, Nadia," said Mama when she came into the room.

She was right. I had been ridiculous. Still, what a relief to vent my feelings for once, to yell and stomp and be alone. My cheeks, still swollen from all the tears I'd shed in the bathroom, felt heavy but refreshed, ready to soldier on. Like me.

I pretended to be asleep. Mama sighed. As she moved back into the salon, I heard her explain to one of my brothers, "She's still upset about Fowzi. Maybe some of us will never get over it." I blocked out the finality of her statement, sticking my fingers in my ears. *He will come back, I'll get him back.* And if I couldn't? Well, then I'd help make them pay.

The next thing I knew, the house was dark and Mama snored softly in the bed next to mine. My resolve had been strengthened. My future stretched out in a straight line: find Walid, get an assignment, launch my career as a member of the revolution.

No longer willing to wait for Walid to contact me, I lay in

bed, thinking up options. First choice: a message via the lame beggar. If he never darkened the traffic light again? Pound the rocky sidewalks of Yarmuk, haunt Walid's hangouts: Tishreen Park, the war museum. Still empty-handed? I'd try more original plans. A sign outside my window, as ridiculous as it was romantic. An ad in the newspaper, however dangerous it might be. Hire a detective, if I had to sell my gold bracelets to do it.

I had decided to get up and pray *istakhara* when I heard a pattern of light raps against the window screen. I caught my breath and looked across at the still-sleeping Mama. If Nassir or Mohammad had forgotten their house key, they'd rattle the front door until someone woke up.

I climbed out of bed. In the time it took me to wrap myself in a robe, cover my head with a scarf, and tiptoe to the window, I heard the pattern of light raps a second time.

My heart pounding, I raised the screen inch by inch. On the path below, outside Auntie Um Suheil's garden, a young man leaned against a garbage can. He wore the gray pants and fitted cap of the city street cleaner. A dark head tipped back and dark brown eyes I knew well stared up at me. A small ball of crumpled paper whizzed through the air and knocked against the edge of the windowsill. I grabbed it before it could tumble back into the garden.

"Nadia?" My mother's groggy voice came from the bed. "Is something wrong?" She flipped over and watched with half-opened eyes as I slid the screen back into place. "Everything's fine," I said. "Just shooing a nasty mosquito out of the room."

She had fallen back asleep already.

I didn't dare uncrumple the paper until I was safe inside the bathroom. In the glare of the overhead light, I read, *Friday. 4:00. Suq al-Hamadiya, the last juice shop before the Omayyad Mosque.*

# In the Name of God,
## the Propitious

On Friday, I was desperate enough to use the Auntie Um Noah excuse. Nassir stared at me with raised eyebrows. "You've never wanted to visit Auntie Um Noah in your life," he said. I had enough reputation left that he didn't question my truthfulness. "Is this some kind of penance?"

"To get out the last time, I had to promise I'd come again. I'll be home before Mama gets back from Auntie Um Fowzi's."

*Suq al-Hamadiya* was the perfect place to arrange a meeting, if it had to be on a Friday. Not crowded, but enough confused foreigners wandering around, and enough greedy shopkeepers open on a day of rest, that I didn't stick out. Most of the juice shops near the Omayyad Mosque were in service, and as I approached the closest one, I saw Walid standing there. He wore a *galabiya* with gold trim on the edge, leather sandals, and a white prayer cap. In each hand, he held a glass of juice.

"I only have ten minutes," I told him up front.

He indicated the courtyard of the mosque. "And *salaam aleikum* to you, too."

"*Aleikum salaam*," I said, my face flushing. I did that much too often around him. We walked toward the open gates of the mosque and he handed me a glass. "Sorry, I'm in such a hurry. I need to get all the way out to Midan and back. . . ."

"You don't need to apologize," he said, lifting one hand. Was it the urgency of the afternoon or did he really look more handsome in traditional prayer clothes?

I took a sip of juice. Orange and strawberry and another fruit I didn't recognize. Although the Friday sermon and afternoon prayers had been over for several hours, men still milled about, most of them in *galabiyas* and prayer caps. The Omayyad Mosque might be a safe place for a girl to meet a boy, but it was a perilous spot to discuss conspiracy theories.

"I'm glad you came," he said. "I—well, I've changed my mind."

I took another sip, still trying to identify the elusive fruit. "What do you mean 'changed your mind?'"

He drained his glass. "I don't want to be involved with you anymore." He flashed a quick glance around and his voice was so low I had to stare at his lips to make out what he said. "Everything's changed. I'm sorry." He passed the glass back to the juice-stand operator and whirled on his heel, disappearing into the crowd.

*Not this time.* I put my half-drunk glass of juice on the counter of the wooden stand and it slopped onto my hand. Then I pushed my way through the mass of bodies coming toward me.

Most of the men were taller than I was, but I managed to keep Walid's moving head in sight. I didn't have much time to analyze my emotions, but I know I felt fear—fear that I'd never see him again, that all my sneaking around had been in vain. Anger that he'd treated me like a lovesick teenager. Bewilderment—hadn't he arranged this meeting, after all? But mostly I felt determined. Steady of purpose, filled with resolve, certain that my course was the true path. Like the Prophet.

He rounded the corner, and I rounded it right behind him. I saw him glance over his shoulder at me. The crowded *suq* worked to my advantage; he couldn't break into a run without calling attention to himself.

Another corner, a café—loud men shouting over their late-afternoon backgammon games. I didn't need a warning to remember that the cafés of Damascus are full of spies. We passed through the glass *suq*, hand-blown lamps hanging in the windows, and through the antiquities market, where Visa and MasterCard stickers adorned the doors. Around the bend, twist, twist, a second alley. I'd never find my way back. Then we were out of the *suq* altogether, skirting the edge of the towering wall that had once enclosed a medieval city. A light changed and a line of motorcars streamed through an intersection, leaving Walid stranded on a corner. I caught up to him. My face was hot and angry; in the moment it took me to catch my breath, he spoke.

"Well, I can't say it's easy to shake you."

"What the devil do you mean by this? Meet me at this time and in this place, sneak out of your house, lie to your family, and then, sorry, it's over. I'm not some romantic schoolgirl, you know. I'm as serious about this as you are."

There was no one to hear us except stone walls, but he whispered anyway. "Someone spoke to Fowzi. I got word this afternoon."

Under the powerful summer sun, I went cold.

"He's fine," Walid added. The traffic light changed, cars screeched to a halt. "If not exactly fine, he's alive and breathing. It looks like he'll be in for some time, may God protect him."

Across the street, the proprietor of the only open store, a corner shop, chased out a small boy who was stuffing an orange into his mouth. "Go," he shouted, waving a stick over his head. "Get out of here! *Animal!*"

I licked my dry lips. "Who spoke with him?"

Walid looked over my head, staring at the stone wall behind me. "He said a cousin of his turned him in. Which makes everything a million times more dangerous, especially for you."

Bassam. Rage flooded through me, my stomach clenched, my teeth ground down. My hands shook. I clasped them together and the palms trembled. "So what?" I said. "I knew that all along."

"You did?" His eyes met mine, almost for the first time. Eyes brown and admiring. "You know who it is?"

"Someone who sold his soul to the West a long time ago. This time he got gold for it—a visa to America." It made so much sense.

"He knows you support Fowzi?"

"Everyone supports Fowzi. And this traitor, he thinks I'm a silly little girl." Especially after my breakdown the other day. Giving way to my anger and pain seemed part of a grand master plan now. And God is the best of planners.

Walid dug his hand into his black hair, slid his face into his elbow. A flicker of light and traffic roared through the intersection, an open pickup truck spewing exhaust in our direction.

Reaching into the side pocket of his flowing *galabiya*, Walid brought out a crumpled piece of notebook paper. He smoothed it out, stared at it long enough that the light changed again. "Can you buy these things for us?" he asked me, still looking at the paper. "Get them at different stores, where the owners have seen you before but don't know you well enough to talk to you. Keep them somewhere nobody can find them. Meet me next Friday, two p.m., same place."

He held the list between his two fingers, without moving, as though he wasn't sure he wanted to give it to me. I could yet walk away. Not sneak around, not tell lies to my family, not come back next Friday. Be as innocent as the day I first saw him. Except I knew the truth now: none of us is innocent in this world.

I reached out my hand and took the list.

# In the Name of God, the Lord of Majesty and Bounty

I made my way past mounds of piled wires, shelves packed with computer equipment, and a pair of huge speakers on the floor. A small black-and-white TV had been mounted behind the counter of the electronics shop, and the clerk stood with his back to me, watching al-Jazeera. A finance program with an Arab hostess I didn't recognize and the Japanese minister of tourism. "Did you ever think it would get to this point?" she asked him.

No, I didn't. An unassuming place, this shop, to launch my most important journey. It shouldn't have set my heart pounding, but it did. "Excuse me," I said.

The clerk whirled around. He was a young man, in his twenties, with a silver chain around his neck. "*Salaam aleikum,*" he said.

"*Aleikum salaam.*" I took a piece of white notebook paper out of my pocket and unfolded it. "My brother sent me to buy this— he was afraid I'd forget, but my memory's not that bad. Still, he wrote it down for me." I handed him a square of paper where I'd copied Walid's first ingredient in a boyish hand.

The clerk looked at it and nodded. "What's he making— some kind of radio?"

I raised both hands in a know-nothing pose. "I have no idea," I said. "He locks himself in his room with electrical stuff and three months later comes out with some household gadget. Never works, though."

The clerk nodded again. He moved out from behind the counter and began pushing aside the electrical cords coiled on the nearest shelf.

"I'm glad you came in," he said. "My first sale of the day."

"Business is bad?"

"It's been better." He found a stool and dragged it against the shelf. Climbing up, he added, "I'm trying to emigrate." He found the correct wires, all of them red, and carried them back to the counter. "I have a cousin in Canada; he says it's great there, except the winters are bone cold. Six feet of snow, can you imagine? You have to wear a mask that covers your whole face when you go out." He laughed. "My cousin says in the winters everyone's a *hijabi*. That will be, let me see, 200 lira."

I handed across my lunch money for the week.

"Thank you," he said. "God be with you, sister."

"And with you." I put the plastic bag with the wires deep inside my backpack. Then I headed out the door.

# In the Name of God, the Enricher

I stared into the shop window. Two household drills sat side by side in dusty boxes: large, six thousand lira; small, thirty-five hundred lira. I pressed my lips together and headed down the street without a backward glance. Around the corner, past a *shawarma* shop, a juice stand, a store selling cheap lingerie for married women. Funny to think I'd once been afraid to come to Yarmuk alone.

I pushed through the glass door and found myself in a tiny room. A shabby green couch lined the back wall, leaving just enough space for a display case and the man seated on a stool behind it. He looked up from the Qur'an he'd been reading. "*Salaam aleikum.*"

"*Aleikum salaam.*"

"Can I help you?"

I reached my hand into my pocket and pulled out the velvet bag Bassam had brought me from the Emirates years ago. Opening it, I spilled the crescent necklace onto the counter. "I want to sell this," I said.

He stared at the necklace for a minute, then picked it up and rubbed the gold between his fingers. Inch by inch, he examined each section of chain, and spent extra time on the crescent itself. "Not made locally, was it?"

I raised my eyebrows. In foreign films, that's a question mark; here it means no.

"Somewhere in the Gulf, I'd guess, Oman maybe, or the Emirates." He looked up at me, but I didn't answer. "It's yours to sell?"

That got my attention. "Are you calling me a thief?" I almost held out my hand for the necklace. Plenty of gold shops lined the streets of Yarmuk.

"Of course not. But a young girl like you—does your father know you're selling this?"

I tapped my fingers against his glass countertop. Underneath, a set of plastic trays held gold rings, brooches, pendants. Letters of the alphabet, English and Arabic, in ornate calligraphy. Swords of Ali for the Alawi, crosses for the Christians, and pendants spelling out the name Allah for the rest of us. "My father's dead," I said. "Mama and I have to survive somehow."

Sympathy flickered in his dark eyes. "Of course," he said. I'd told the truth, but I felt a stab of guilt anyway. Lying's in the intent, isn't it? And I would have said my father was living on Mars, if it would further my cause.

"Times are hard for everybody these days," he added. "The war, and the sanctions, and the uncertainty. We get twice as many people selling gold now as buying it." He lifted a tiny scale out from under the counter and placed it beside my necklace. "I can only pay you for the weight, you know. Not the work, though it looks like it's been done by a master craftsman. Probably a lot less than you paid for it."

"It was a gift," I said. "And we have to eat." Again, the truth. Again, the twinge.

He put my necklace on the scale. It weighed in at .8 grams. "I can give you forty-five hundred lira for it."

Forty-five hundred. More than enough for the small drill, which came in at number two on Walid's list. A week ago, a few days ago, I might have felt some kind of regret as the gold seller slipped the pendant off my necklace and dropped it in one of the trays, as the chain became just another gold chain on a metal rack. After all, it was the only expensive thing I'd ever owned.

Today I felt only relief that I'd rid myself of the gift of a vile traitor. And pride at my own resourcefulness. Walid hadn't given me any money for the things I'd been told to collect, no suggestions on how to get them. Yet I'd found a way.

The gold seller placed the money on the counter. "Here's a little extra," he said, adding a few hundred lira. "The Prophet gave in charity to widows and orphans. Go with God."

No twinge this time. The Prophet also gave in the cause of the Muslims. These days, I was grateful for any sign God sent my way. I scooped the money off the counter and hid it in the inside pocket of my purse. "God be with you, too." On the wings of angels, I walked out of the shop.

# In the Name of God, the Most High, the Sublime

Trying to keep the skip out of my step, I entered the house-wares shop. Larger than the goldsmith's, this store had a center counter supporting a rack filled with candy bars, packets of biscuits, and tiny plastic toys. A Pepsi cooler stood beside the rack. Small appliances lined the shelves along the far wall, inter-rupted by knives, wooden spoons, and other utensils hanging on a bit of pinboard. The candy seemed to be selling, but a thick layer of dust covered everything else.

The shopkeeper leaned against the sheet of glass that served as a countertop, rocking on his elbows. On the other side of the counter, two men sat on stools, cups of cooled tea in front of them.

The shopkeeper bent his head around them and greeted me. *"Salaam aleikum."*

*"Aleikum salaam.* I'm looking for a small drill, the kind you'd use to fix household appliances. The man at the hardware store said I might find one here."

The men on the stools stared for a moment, then turned back to their tea.

"We have a few like that," said the shopkeeper, moving out from behind the counter and crossing the room to take two bat-tered boxes off the shelf. "This one is Russian; it has a revolu-tionary propeller design. And this is from China—not as long lasting as the Japanese models, but much cheaper."

I fiddled with the ends of my scarf. "I noticed some in the

window on my way into the store; they looked more like what I want."

"Those are the Japanese models." He tilted his head to one side. "They cost almost twice as much."

"But they'll last longer, right?"

He put the boxes back on the shelf and headed toward the window. I watched him shift boxes with a long wooden pole. This was really happening. In a few minutes, the box would be mine. In a few days, I'd be handing the materials over to Walid, no longer a helpless girl who wished the world was different, a girl who watched TV in silent horror and wept in the bathroom.

I'd be a girl who made things happen. I already was.

"Large or small?" called out the shopkeeper.

I had to go with what I could afford. "Small."

The shopkeeper used a long wooden pole to pull my new drill from the front of the window. Then he crossed back to the counter, where he filled out a slip of paper. "That's thirty-five hundred lira," said the shopkeeper.

I counted out the bills. New dilemma: this box was not going to fit in my backpack. How on earth would I smuggle it into the house? "It's a present for my brother," I said. "Could you wrap it in brown paper?"

The shopkeeper sighed, but he fumbled under the counter till he came up with sheets of paper, and then did as I asked, slapping tape all over the package. Without prompting, he placed the entire thing in a large plastic bag. I had the whole trip home to think of an explanation, but by the time I reached the door of the shop, I'd already found one: a present from Miss to her brother, but she didn't want to keep it at home in case he stumbled across it. I'd volunteered to keep it for her until the weekend.

Resourceful. That's me.

# In the Name of God, the Compeller

The line was taking forever. At last the round Kurdish woman wrapped up her argument with the pharmacist and stormed out the door. I tapped my foot. Mama would believe it took only so long to buy potatoes.

"I thought that was you." She had to say my name twice before I realized she was talking to me. I spun around. Samira.

"Don't you usually go to Dudi's?" Across the street from our building, Dudi's Pharmacy is small and disorganized, with half-full bottles strewn across the counters. His kind heart—and his credit— more than makes up for the confusion, though. Al-Mansouri Pharmacy is sparkling clean with swept floors and drugs kept in locked cabinets, but it's twice the price.

"They were out of what I need." What was I going to say when she asked me what I needed? "What are you doing here?"

"I saw you through the window and I thought, that looks like Nadia. So I came inside to see." She slipped her backpack off her shoulders and let it drop to her side. "I'll wait with you if you like."

I didn't like. "You don't have to."

"I'm glad I found you here, actually," said Samira. There had to be some way to get rid of her. Ask her to take the potatoes home to Mama? Then Mama would want to know what I was doing in the pharmacy. "I want to tell you something, and it's hard to find a private place to do it."

"What?" Maybe I could ask her to buy something I'd forgotten. Parsley? Onions? Lemons?

The young soldier in front of us turned around and stared at Samira. With every wisp of hair covered by her scarf, she was still striking—especially with pink lip gloss shining her lips, color dusting her eyes and cheeks.

"I applied to that program in Geneva."

Whatever. "You said you were going to."

"I said I might. Now I have. I know you don't approve—you think I'm going to lose my religion over there, but it's not about that. I want to make a difference, Nadia, and there's no room to do that here."

What did Samira know about making a difference?

I stared at the floor. How could I ask for test tubes with Samira standing beside me? A project for school? But suppose she mentioned it to someone, Nassir or Mama or, worst of all, Bassam?

I could hear the gossip already. "What does she want with test tubes?" "Test tubes? Do you suppose she's making a love potion?" "Nadia? More like a wrath of God potion." Eventually some clever person would put two and two together. "You don't suppose Nadia's trying to make a bomb, do you?" The government wouldn't matter if Mama got me first.

Samira prattled on about her chances for the internship. "Anyway," she finished. "That's not what I wanted to tell you." She paused. Maybe I could pretend to see a neighbor outside and send Samira careening after her?

"It's Yasmine, actually," she said. "Well, Yasmine and Bassam. They're engaged. There, I've said it."

Was that why Yasmine had dropped her lover? She'd found someone better, someone who could take her to America? Someone who had betrayed her brother to do it. My heart went cold. Even Yasmine wasn't as shallow as that. "She can't marry Bassam."

I looked up to find Samira staring at me. "I would have said you never cared two pins about Bassam. Or is it your vanity that's affected? Come, Cousin, be generous."

What to say? *Bassam's the one who betrayed Fowzi to the secret police*. How do I know? Because a revolutionary Islamicist told me. How do I know him? Oh, I meet him on random street corners when I'm supposed to be in school.

My eyes filled with tears. Impossible to tell the truth. Impossible to come up with a credible lie.

"You're really upset over this, aren't you? Were you hiding a crush on Bassam all this time?"

The soldier in front of us had reached the head of the line. He was whispering, but I heard snatches of his dilemma—"personal problem . . . every night . . . can't afford to marry for years."

"Bassam's nothing to me. Nothing." I took hold of myself, did my best to sweep the bitterness out of my mouth. "I can't stand the thought of one more member of my family drowning in the cesspool of the West."

"And you're crying over that?"

"I'm not crying." For the rest of my life, I'll be known as the girl who wanted Bassam and couldn't have him.

*"Salaam aleikum,"* said the pharmacist. "How can I help you?"

Another person I had no answer for.

Samira nudged me. "Nadia," she said. "It's your turn."

Inspiration struck. "Well, it's just that, um, I've been a bit itchy." I flashed an embarrassed look in Samira's direction. "It's hard to describe, but . . ."

"Oh," said Samira. Her cheeks wore that bloodstained look. "I'll meet you outside, Nadia." She moved to the back of the pharmacy and the door banged shut behind her. The tactful pharmacist had already reached under the counter and brought forth an unlabeled white jar.

I cleared my throat. "I'm sorry—what I told you wasn't exactly right." My shame played well as a cover. "The thing is, my cousin, her family isn't doing well. Her brother, he lost his job. We need test tubes for an important chemistry experiment at school, and my cousin, she just doesn't have the money for them."

The pharmacist had disappeared into the back of the shop before I finished my sentence. Within minutes, he returned with a small package wrapped in brown paper. I took out the roll of money left over after yesterday's drill purchase and handed him several hundred-lira bills.

"May God reward you for your kindness," said the pharmacist.

If he only knew. I left the pharmacy filled with pleasure at outwitting Samira. A million things might happen before Yasmine took the final step of marrying the man who'd destroyed her brother. An explosion in downtown Damascus, for example.

# In the Name of God,
## the Last,
# He Whose Existence Is Without End

 *"Salaam aleikum."*

*"Aleikum salaam."*

"Do you sell ball bearings?"

"Ball bearings? What does a pretty young lady want with oil and grease?"

"My brother asked me to pick some up. Do you have any?"

"Your brother sent you all the way to Baromka to get ball bearings? What, he's a cripple?"

"I was visiting relatives in Midan, and he asked me if I'd stop in on the way home. He has the car all to pieces and he didn't want to leave. Do you have any ball bearings?"

"For his car?"

No answer.

"Times are hard these days, when a man can't afford to take his car to a mechanic. Ten to one he'll mess the wiring so bad he'll wish he never started. He trained in cars?"

Pause. "No."

"He hard up? I could give you a cut rate."

"We're fine, thank you. He likes to work on cars."

"Really? He in the market for something new?"

No answer.

"You seem to be a nice girl. You married?"

"If you don't have any ball bearings, I'll try the next shop."

"I'm looking for them."

"Not to be rude, but most people, when they look for things,

PAULA JOLIN

actually get up and look around."

"No, I'm looking in my head, trying to remember where I put them."

No answer.

"That's what I want, a nice, religious girl, proper dress, eyes in her head where they belong, not staring at pictures of men in tight pants. Not so many of you left."

"Only God will judge."

"I've got eyes. My family's pushing me to get married, but the girl my aunt suggests, she's flighty. Likes to listen to music and giggle in corners."

"Girls aren't always what they seem."

"You think I should take her?"

"I think it would be nice if you could remember where you put those ball bearings."

"Right here. You need eight boxes?"

"Eight."

"That's sixteen hundred lira."

"Sixteen hundred?"

"Is that a problem? I could, uh, maybe offer you a discount."

"I'll take six then."

"Six? I could give you the eight for fourteen fifty. A special deal for you. And then we could have a nice cup of tea, discuss proper manners, give me some tips for this girl. . . ."

"I'll take six, thank you."

# In the Name of God, the Creator

Baromka to home on foot would take me close to an hour. With the last of my money in the hands of the mechanic, I had no choice. Brief fantasy: Walid whizzes by in a sports car and stops at the corner, waiting for me. His hair is a bit wild, from driving with the top down. "Get in, Nadia," he says. "Would you like to drive?" To the nearby shopkeeper with the bushy eyebrows shooting up into his hairline, he says, "Don't look so scandalized. She's my wife."

Back to reality. Put one foot in front of the other, Nadia, and you can make it home. Mama wouldn't be expecting me till six, since I'd offered to return her book to Auntie Um Noah. I'd gone there right after school, rapped softly on the door, left the book on the welcome mat—and I was ready for investigation, if it came. "I knocked and knocked, Mama, but no one answered. Maybe Auntie needs a hearing aid."

If Mama even asked. We'd been avoiding each other for days, but last night, after I came home from the pharmacy, she cornered me in the kitchen. "Nadia, can we talk? I know you don't think I'm much use to you these days, but believe it or not, I understand a little about broken hearts."

"My heart is fine." A part of me, a small part perhaps, but a part still there, wiggled its way up through the queasiness of my stomach, the hard space in my chest. A part that wanted to burst into tears, throw myself into my mother's arms, ask her to teach me how to be kind. A part that was overwhelmed by the rest of me. I said, "You of all people know what I think of Bassam. And Yasmine. They deserve each other."

Mama looked at me for a long time. It occurred to me that maybe she hadn't meant Bassam at all, but the alternative was too painful to think about. She dried her hands on a kitchen towel. "Oh, Nadia," she said. There was a moment, a single moment, when things could have gone her way. How nice to love her once again! In the living room, someone flicked on the TV; as often happens, the voice went extra loud. CNN, talking about the war. America, invading my life again. "Oh, Mama," I said, and the ice in my heart floated into colder waters.

Yesterday, we hadn't exchanged one word, and this morning, I didn't see her before I left for the day. Later events crowded my mind: school, Auntie Um Noah's, taking the bus to Baromka, buying the ball bearings. Now the long walk home, still two miles to go.

Fantasy No. 2: Sit at the side of the road and pretend to be a beggar. Moan, *"For the sake of God, for the sake of the Prophet,"* until someone takes pity and gives me bus fare. In favor: I'd get to sit down and I'd get to help someone fulfill their religious duty to give charity. Against: If anyone I knew saw me, the pavement and I would part company for a long time. Properly raised Muslim girls don't do things like beg in the street. Neither, of course, do properly raised boys. That brought my thoughts back to Walid.

What did he do in the many days and hours I didn't see him? Stationed himself inside cafés to overhear rumors, I assumed, met shady characters in abandoned buildings, led his double life. Maybe he even had a job. Engineer, perhaps, or architect. Something in an office, his slender hands drawing complicated documents. Not a doctor, somehow I was sure of that. He'd be too apt to tell the patients to stop whining and get some exercise.

For a moment, I indulged in fantasy again. Sneaking around the city, collecting items for the cause, I felt closer to God than I ever had. His words echoed in my heart. These small steps to glory, to change, they were my first real venture down the straight path. Still, a moment of fantasy couldn't hurt, could it? Walid knocks on the door of our apartment, demands to see Mohammad. I'm in the bedroom with Mama, the door ajar enough to listen, and she's her old self, giggly, squeezing my hand, whispering *nice legs*! Improper of course, but the scene so exciting, we might be forgiven for once. Mohammad wants to know everything about Walid, starting with how he plans to support me. "I want Nadia to continue her studies after the wedding," Walid tells him. "I wouldn't be happy if my wife wasn't using the gifts God gave her." A shiver runs through me at the words *my wife* and Mama's grip on my hand tightens enough to break it.

The pretending lasted until I reached home. Mama bustling around the kitchen, Nassir and Mohammad shouting at each other in the salon, pulled me out of my reverie. It wasn't a time for dreaming anyway. I had work to do.

# In the Name of God, the Witness

It must have been after midnight. Lights off, doors closed, the wooden wall clock marking time across the room. No rain threatened this time, but that sense of something wrong I'd had the day I'd found Nassir alone in the darkened apartment, I had that same sense now. Impending doom.

I got up on bare feet and crossed to the window, where I lifted the shade in silence, making *dua* against a squeak. I leaned out the window, stared into the street. Then:

"Nadia?" The voice came from the balcony. After one second of thinking a burglar had broken in, I identified it as Nassir's. "What are you doing?"

Cornered, I approached the truth. "I thought I heard someone outside," I said. "How come you're still awake?"

God backed me up. "It was probably me, coming out here," said Nassir. His voice still sounded strange, not like him. "I'm sorry," he said. "Go back to sleep."

"Nassir? Are you—are you crying?"

"I'm fine."

I walked out onto the balcony. My heart battered the inside of my chest. "Is something the matter? What happened?" I hadn't heard Nassir cry since our father died. "Is it Fowzi?"

"Is it Fowzi?" Nassir made a sound, something like the bray of a donkey, but I think he meant it as a laugh. "You might say that."

"What do you mean?" Bile rose in my throat. "Is he—"

"It's not Fowzi," said Nassir. "It's me. I didn't get the job."

"Oh." I came full out onto the balcony in my nightgown, hair tumbling over my shoulders. There was no light; it would take an astronomer to see my state of undress. Distress. Nassir sat in a metal fold-out chair beside the balcony railing and I opened a matching chair and joined him. Reaching for his hand would have been too much, but I softened my voice. "Nassir, I'm so sorry."

"Don't, Nad." We'd been children the last time he called me that, racing each other to the kitchen for the first piece of cake. "I can't bear it, sympathy, right now."

"Sure."

We sat in silence so long that my eyes closed. A deep sense of loss pervaded me, for Nassir, for us all. Nassir might have paid for Dimah and Mariam's school, helped Mohammad and Sarah buy a house, gotten Mama some nice clothes for once.

"After everything I've done," said Nassir. He spoke quietly, so quietly I leaned forward to listen. "All these years looking for jobs, I mean. I was so sure . . . ."

"What happened?"

"How would I know?" He lowered his head, making his voice harder to hear. "I do know. They decided to go with someone else. 'You're a very qualified candidate, Nassir, but you must know there are many qualified candidates out there. I wish we had jobs for all of you.'"

"A woman?" I held my breath.

"An Alawi."

I folded my arms over my chest. "I want to say 'Don't worry about it, you'll find something else,' but I'd smack you if you said that to me, if I were in your position, I mean. So I don't know what to say. Except that I'm your sister and I love you, and I'll love you if you take a job selling hamburgers."

"Or alcohol?"

"But you wouldn't—"

"One chance in two years," he said. "And now going to the Gulf is out of the question. Mohammad was supposed to look around for me, and now he's not even there." His fingers gripped the bottom of his chair and he rocked backward. "Nadia, why do you hate Bassam so much?"

"Funny you should say that; Samira seems to think I'm in love with him."

"If she does, she's blind. Really Nad—why do you hate him so much?"

A breeze blew across the balcony and lifted the hair off the back of my neck. It felt strange to be half-undressed, even in the dark. "I don't hate Bassam. I just—we're totally different people, that's all. He's materialistic and not, I don't know, not God oriented. No one believes this, but I think he and Yasmine are unsuited. If she knew—if she knew what was good for her, she'd marry someone religious, someone who could lead her in the right direction."

"It's not like they're making you marry him." Nassir studied my face. "Why get so upset about it? You don't even like Yasmine."

"She's my cousin," I said. "And a *Muslimah*."

"Is it about Fowzi?"

I felt the cold discomfort of the metal chair beneath my thin nightgown, the scrape of the cement balcony as I brushed my toes across its rough surface. "Is what about Fowzi?"

"Is that why you're mad at Bassam? Do you think he had something to do with Fowzi's arrest?"

I thought about lying. But here on the balcony, alone in the dark with the brother who'd been so deeply wounded, I didn't want to pretend. I wanted to shout the truth to the four corners of the earth, I wanted to tear down the block of lies that made people like Mama think *what a nice guy*. I wanted someone else to know that Yasmine was about to build her marriage on a bedrock of betrayal. "I know he did. Someone, I can't tell you who, someone said they knew someone who talked to Fowzi in prison. Thirdhand, I know, but—"

"Someone in the family? No one would spread a rumor like that."

"This person said Fowzi told him it was Bassam who turned him in. And it fits in with everything else—Bassam's 'friend' who found him a job in the States, his almost miraculous visa at a time when the U.S. is kicking Muslims out, not letting them in. Bassam sold Fowzi out for a chance in the States, and he'll never look back." I sat back in my chair with a thud. "And that's why I don't like him."

Another long silence flitted across the balcony rail with the breeze. Gentle and kind, peace and wind wrapped themselves around me, as though the night respected my decision to share my suspicions. If I had died without speaking, Bassam's hypocrisy would go unchecked.

"It wasn't Bassam," said Nassir. "It was me."

Gentle left the balcony. "Don't try to defend him—"

"I'm not defending anyone. Do you think I'm that stupid? I knew you thought that about Bassam, and I thought, it doesn't matter, he's going to go off to America and marry Yasmine and live happily ever after, what difference does it make? Tonight, though, everything shattered, knowing I did it for nothing . . . somehow it seems to matter after all."

I couldn't quite get my mind around his words. I heard him speak but he made no sense. "Are you saying that you betrayed Fowzi for a job? Are you trying to protect Bassam—"

Nassir took both my hands in his and shook them. "This has nothing to do with Bassam! For once, just once, could you put your preconceived ideas aside? Could you see the world as it is, not as it's ordered in that head-in-the-clouds of yours? Try. Bassam doesn't pray equals bad, Nassir prays equals good. Except it doesn't always work that way."

He dropped my hands, turned his head aside. "I was desperate, Nadia. You don't know what it's like, what a failure I feel. Every chance at a job—gone. Lost. Given to someone else. I kept thinking the same things over and over again. Why couldn't I find a job? What would I do if I didn't have Mama's house to live in?"

I stared into my lap. In the silence that echoed louder than words, I said, "I wouldn't betray someone to the secret police if I was being ground into the dirt by pigs' hooves."

"You don't know what you'd do until you do it. I was talking with Mahmoud the night after the picnic—I know you don't like him, but he's the one person I know who might get me a job. We went to hang out with some friends of his, and one of them is the son of the minister of defense. An Alawi. I asked him about jobs and he brushed me off. Then we started talking about insurgents, and the danger of them spreading here." The shadows made it impossible for me to see Nassir's face, but I couldn't miss the tremble in his voice.

"'Nassir's just this side of an insurgent,' Mahmoud said. 'Hardly likely,' said this Alawi guy. All the others were drinking. I wasn't, but I hadn't left, I guess that's why he figured I wasn't that strict. And then he started talking about a group of insurgents, one of them, the most dangerous one, was speaking out against the government in public, claiming that only an Islamic state could guarantee justice.

"I said—and I swear, Nadia, I didn't think before I spoke, I said, 'That sounds like my cousin Fowzi.' And this Alawi guy said, 'Really? You interest me very much.'"

My hands were clenching my thighs, digging into the soft skin underneath my nightgown. "Nassir—how could you?"

"The next day, Fowzi was picked up."

I took a deep breath. My spinning head made it impossible to comprehend what I'd heard. "Maybe it was a coincidence. You said yourself you didn't mean to say it, maybe—"

"Who's defending people now?"

I had no words to answer that. No defense.

Nassir spoke again. "Who, in this country, doesn't think before they speak? In the company of an Alawi? I can say that, but I know the truth: I was indiscreet on purpose. Subconscious, maybe, but still on purpose. There was a thought in my head: if I work with this guy, he'll work with me. And he did. A few weeks after Fowzi, he called me and said he had an opening for an ambitious, helpful guy like me."

"So Bassam never got you that job?"

"Don't blame Bassam. I didn't want anyone to know it came through Mahmoud. So I, well, I lied about it. I knew no one would bother to trace it."

That same breeze now seemed sinister and cold. I tightened my arms across my chest. My body felt heavy, as though I'd shed enough tears to sink an ocean liner, and suddenly I couldn't stand to share the same slab of balcony concrete with Nassir, to breathe the same air.

I stood up, pushing the chair with the backs of my knees. "I'm going to bed." He waited until I reached the door before he asked me, "Are you going to tell people? I wouldn't blame you, but I, well, I wish you wouldn't."

"I don't know what I'm going to do."

# In the Name of God,
## the Restorer,
## the Giver of Life

I lied. I knew exactly what I was going to do.

I closed the door behind me, leaving Nassir stranded on the balcony. I took down my prayer rug and spread it out, then headed to the washroom to perform my ablutions. Returning, I prayed *istakhara*. I prayed *istakhara* as I had never prayed before, with fervency and devotion but somehow simply, too. By the end, the one word *God* was enough, consuming me in my silence, devouring me with its fire. I am a plain human being, with no pretense to be anything more, but in that name, I caught something, I think, of how the Prophet prayed.

May God forgive me if what I have said is blasphemous.

I climbed into bed and pulled the bedsheet over my head. I wasn't thinking of anything. Not of Nassir's betrayal, not of Fowzi's payment in hard currency, not even of the doubts that slid through the cracks in my anger. *Are you so much more loyal? Haven't you forgotten Fowzi yourself, forgotten that once you meant to marry him? And now you're thinking of someone else.* I know it's impossible to think of nothing, but I was, and thinking of everything, all at once. I was thinking about God.

*Should I demand to set off the bomb myself?* That was the question I'd asked God to answer, the yes or no I'd sought when I said my prayer. By the time the cool sheets met my face, I knew what He would say. I couldn't imagine my reception in heaven, that would be wrong, putting a face to things beyond human knowledge. But I could imagine the effects on those left behind.

CNN, reporting from the scene of the explosion: "It appears it was a girl who launched this attack, Mowry. A young girl, seventeen or eighteen years old, we don't have further details." Al-Jazeera: "Nineteen foreigners were killed by a suicide bomber in Damascus today, prompting the startled government to reassess its security. The first suicide bombing to take place on Syrian soil, this has led many Islamic leaders to claim that all the earth is a battlefield." CNN again: "Today's suicide bombing is forcing the American military to reconsider its position on Iraqi insurgents. A seventeen-year-old girl set off a bomb in Syria to make the point that no Muslims will be oppressed under the weight of American combat boots."

Closer to home, my family would sit around the television, mouths hanging open. Mohammad would be appalled. Nassir would think I'd done it out of disgust for his confession. Mama . . . well, I could place Mama's reaction exactly, I'd seen it so many times. She would cry and wring her hands and bemoan the future—as she had when Mohammad lost his job—and then she'd dry her tears and make some tea.

My motive, pure love of God, couldn't drown out the knowledge that there were organizations that helped the families of *jihadis*. I pictured Mama opening the front door and finding a green check with lots of zeroes under the welcome mat. Or, to keep it anonymous, a thick brown envelope stuffed with cash.

The fortune, the survival, of our family would no longer depend on my brothers' hopeless job searches. Mohammad and Sarah could save their marriage in a new apartment, Mama could pay the gas bill and still have meat for dinner. Nassir could buy a future that wouldn't make him betray his family.

Compensation or no compensation, my action would reverberate beyond our apartment. The *hijabi* girls at school would never stop speculating. "I knew it," someone would say, "the way she held her head, her pious indifference to worldly problems. I knew her heart was with God." The schoolyard would fill with girls, arms tied with black bands, faces streaked with tears, one or two carrying my picture.

Fowzi, in that cell I could never imagine, would hear the news—maybe from the same unknown who brought out word that his cousin had betrayed him . . . oh. How stupid of me. His cousin. Not Bassam, but Nassir. Or had Fowzi jumped to the same conclusions I had? Surely, if the secret police told him Nassir was the culprit, he would have damned them as liars? Either way, I hoped that Fowzi would understand why I did it and be pleased. Maybe he would lie awake and think, *Nadia followed in my footsteps. What a sister-in-Islam she was.*

Would there be disapproval? Yes, of course. The government, for one. They would issue a stern repressive statement or, worse, try to make me into a creature of shame. "This pathetic young woman who destroyed property and took innocent lives suffered from severe depression." They wouldn't use the word *pregnancy,* but they'd be happy to imply it. When no one believed them, that would be one more black mark against the government.

The West, for another, would be horrified. Shrill talk-show hosts would use me as an example of the depravity of Islam. "It transforms teenage girls into heartless murderers." Around and around they'd go. "Killer babies," "Guerilla girls," "Must be stopped." A few—maybe just a few, but growing in number every day—commentators would note, "If we pulled our troops out, if we stopped interfering with their politics, if we ended support for Israel, these girls could go back to being quiet and oppressed."

West-obsessed scholars might condemn me, too. "There is no killing in Islam, except in self-defense." But the Syrian people, the Arab people, the Muslim Nation would stand up for me. This is self-defense. Community defense. Defense of our lifestyle, our truth, our religion. Our ability to lead the lives that God commands. To find work, to marry, to raise families that aren't harassed and intimidated.

I couldn't imagine, of course, my reward or my punishment in heaven. That would be infringing on God's omnipotence. But . . . if there was a picture in my head of two revolutionaries together, and one of them had dark hair and dark eyes and a slim build, well, I wasn't saying that would be heaven. Even if, in some secular sense, it would.

I don't remember finally falling asleep. I can't say, of course, that I had a smile on my face. But I know that from the moment I understood God's purpose for me, I felt content, sure in the knowledge that I was loved. By God.

# In the Name of God, the Alive

Two small boys tumbled into me, fighting over a football. Another clomped by on the back of a donkey, shouting over his shoulder, "Change money lady, change money?" and a fourth boy trailed behind me. "Do I look like someone with foreign money?" I asked. The spell was broken, the boys scattered. I was left, almost alone and unhindered, on the main route of *Suq al-Hamadiya*.

The juice shop. I held my head high when the juice squeezer winked at me. The same man from last week? I couldn't be sure. Four minutes to go. This time I was early, scanning the street, hoping to blend in. Hoping that Walid would come. Crazy schemes aside, I still had no way to contact him. I reached up to pat the bottom of my heavy backpack. I had the goods. He'd be here.

A middle-aged foreign couple approached the juice stand, chattering to each other in a guttural language, maybe German. The man was pointing to the Omayyad Mosque, waving his hand in a fluttery way, saying something insistent. Gawking at our holy places as though we live in a zoo. Then his wife or girlfriend or mistress or whoever turned to the juice seller and began ordering two orange-strawberry mixes in accented Arabic.

"*Salaam aleikum*, Nadia," Walid said. He let his hand rest on my elbow the briefest of moments. "Let's go."

No time to nod. We flew down half-hidden alleys, out through gates in stone walls, and to a street with a waiting blue car. *Don't go anywhere with strangers, Nadia, never talk to unknown men.* The backseat of the car was leather, the air-conditioning made it almost cold to the touch. A Qur'anic verse, low and rhythmic, played on the radio. It was too uncomfortable to wedge myself between the seat and the backpack; with a few awkward movements, I slid it off my back and twisted it around so I held it in my lap. In the front seat, the driver leaned forward over the steering wheel, a baseball cap pulled low on his forehead. I couldn't see his face.

"Did you get everything?" Walid asked.

"You never told me we were going somewhere in a car," I said. I glanced at the driver as he pulled away from the curb. I didn't want him to hear my conversation any more than he wanted me to see his face.

"I'm not taking that bag from you in any public place," said Walid, a stubborn set to his voice, as though he'd argued this many times before. "We've already met once in the *suq*, established that we have some kind of illicit relationship. I mean, they think we have."

"A Muslim should avoid the appearance of evil," said the driver in a gravelly voice. He sounded older than Walid, and like a smoker.

Walid glared at the back of his head. "Were you willing to go into a mechanic shop and ask for ball bearings?" When the other man didn't answer, Walid turned back to me. "This meeting is no different from any other. It's not like we're alone in a closed space; Omar there might not be much to look at, but he functions nicely as a chaperone. You pass over what's in the bag and we take you to whatever address you give us, it's that straightforward. You'll go with God's thanks . . . and mine, of course."

A shiver erupted along my spine. "Harasta," I said.

"I'm not driving all the way out there," said the driver.

"It'll take all of fifteen minutes." Walid turned back to me. "Did you get everything?"

"There's a condition," I said. "Yes, I got everything, but there's a condition." Walid stared down at his knees. The man in the front seat let his breath out in an impatient huff.

"Unbelievable," he said.

"Walid?"

"I'm waiting for you to tell me what you want." Walid's voice was almost inaudible. He was still looking at his knees or his shoes or the floor. Was he thinking, Silly little girl, about to mess up the thing I've worked for my entire life? Or, Taken again, by a greedy witch demanding diamonds and gold?

I'd thought about this moment all morning, while I cleaned my room and picked at the food on the breakfast tray, when I packed my bag and told Mama I'd catch a taxi out to Harasta to help plan Yasmine's engagement party, but I still didn't know what words to use. When the silence stretched so long I expected the driver to curse me any minute, I said, "I want it to be me."

"What?"

"I want it to be me."

"No, I mean, you want what to be you?"

I took a deep breath, forgot the man in the front seat. Prayed *dua* to God—*Please Lord, let me be clear.* "I want to be the one to do the mission. The bombing—I know that's what all this is for, I'm not stupid."

"Little scammer," said the driver. "This is what you get when you—"

Walid talked right over him. "I realize that when you get involved in a situation like this, it's easy to jump in with both feet. But you have to understand what I'm saying—if you were to do this, it would be forever. It would be irresponsible of me not to slow you down, make you think about things. This incident we're talking about, we're talking about tomorrow."

"Why not tell her when and where?" asked the driver. "Give her our home addresses, too. She's already got the make and model of the car, she knows your face."

"She's upright," said Walid, talking through his teeth. "She's offering to die for God and you're worried about her snaking to the secret police?"

I shifted in the seat, letting the backpack rest unprotected in my lap. I pressed my sweaty wrists against the cold seat below me. "It makes sense for it to be me," I said. "When this happens, whether it happens tomorrow or next week, the police aren't stupid. They're going to lift evidence and analyze fragments. They're going to interview people and ask tough questions." My words came out more smoothly now. "They're going to trace it back to me."

"The whole point is, nobody would notice a girl—"

"A girl buying ball bearings? The mechanic tried to talk to me for twenty minutes. I'm probably the only girl who's come into his store all year."

The driver raised the volume on the radio. *"O ye who believe,"* chanted the Qur'an reader. *"Take your precautions, and either go forth in parties or go forth all together. There are certainly among you men who would tarry behind."*

Walid rubbed the fingers of his right hand together. His words drowned out the rest of the verse. "Fine, I was wrong, everyone else was right. I should never have dragged you into this."

I clicked my tongue. "No, you were right. Because I'm a girl, I could ignore the people who talked to me. I didn't give anything away. A guy would have been expected to talk. It was brilliant."

"That's not why he did it," said the driver.

I didn't want to know. "But the point is, they're going to track me down anyway. They're going to track down whoever becomes a martyr. Doesn't it make sense that that should be the same person? From there, they've got no leads to you, no leads to anywhere. It all goes underground."

"Aren't you worried about your family?"

My lips pressed together, hardened. I held steady. "If I was going to worry about them, I should have done it last week," I said. "Syria's not Israel. Nobody's going to destroy their house."

"Maybe not." He was still staring at his shoes, but I could hear the almost smile in his voice. "Although your family will be interrogated—whatever happens. But aren't you worried that they'll be sad? That they'll miss you?"

I pushed aside images of Nassir staring at my useless school-books, Mama sobbing on the couch. "They'll be proud of me," I said, a truth they might not know right away but one that would sustain them through the weeks and years ahead. "What greater use of a life than to give it to God?"

Walid pressed his palms against the tops of his knees. When he spoke, his question was the last thing I expected. "Even your cousin Bassam?"

I should have seen it coming. "Bassam?"

"You didn't think we'd just let it go, did you, Nadia? Surely you didn't want us to?" Tapping his fingers against his kneecaps, he continued, "Fowzi complained enough about his Westernized cousin who's dying to go to the States. It wasn't hard to guess who you were talking about."

"I was wrong. It wasn't Bassam."

"Trying to protect him?"

Protect Bassam? Hardly. But I had to set the record straight. "I have no doubt that Bassam is capable of betraying the whole Muslim Nation. But he didn't betray Fowzi."

Walid stopped drumming and raised one skeptical eyebrow. "You may not think much of him, but family has to stick together."

"This isn't about family." Carefully hidden inside my shoes, my scraped toes still smarted. My thighs were as cold against the leather seats as they had been on the cheap metal chair. And anger slapped against the inside of my chest, crashed into the chambers of my heart. "My brother Nassir, he'd do anything for a job. I told you that before. He's got the skills, the credentials, he just needs someone to take a chance on his potential. Even if that means taking an entry-level job, working up to something that will change the world. I want to tell him, 'Your time will come.' But he won't listen if it's only me saying it. He thinks to get a job, he'll have to make it happen."

Walid was quick. "So he betrayed Fowzi to the government in hopes they'd be so grateful they'd give him a job?" He didn't need my half nod to know he was right. "What a fool."

"This has nothing to do with Nassir." And it didn't. His confession might have been a catalyst, making me realize I couldn't complain about the state of the world if I didn't try to make it better, but he wasn't the reason behind my decision. "This is about me. Whatever my reasons, I'm the best choice, the only one who's not going to lead the police straight to you."

"There's someone who can connect you," said the driver. "The juice seller. You said the same guy works that stand every week. He'll remember seeing you together."

"He never got a look at my face," Walid told him. He frowned. "There are a million *hijabi* girls sneaking out to meet their boyfriends in this city. How would he connect that with a pious girl martyring herself for God?" I felt another thrill, a different one. He was considering my request. I was one step closer to God. "Anyway, I bought juice from the other vendor. The one who was looking at Nadia, he never saw my face."

"We're almost to Harasta," said the driver.

"I told you it wouldn't take long." Walid rubbed his lips together. "Nadia, I don't like this."

I tilted my head and pressed my cheek against the window. "It's the best way. And look at this: if I'm not the bomber, and the police come looking to interrogate me, how do you think that'll go over with Mama? I'll be so grounded I'd rather be in jail." I tried to add a laugh, but it didn't come out. "You can drop me here—my cousins' apartment is down the street, but if anyone sees me getting out of this car . . . ."

The driver slowed down. "Tomorrow," said Walid. "Nine o'clock. We'll meet you in front of the Central Bank of Syria, same car. Be exactly on time, not a minute early, not a minute late. Wear something loose."

I shivered in the backseat. I wasn't used to such cold; we had only ineffective fans at home. In the silence that followed, the words of the Qur'an echoed in the car. "*Those who believe fight in*

*the cause of God. And those who reject Faith fight in the cause of Evil:
So fight against the friends of Satan: feeble indeed is the cunning of
Satan.*"

"May God watch over you," said the driver.

I unlocked the door and opened it. "Tell me something," I
said to Walid. "If it wasn't me, would it have been you?"

"Him?" The driver laughed. "With a wife and two kids to
support?"

Walid glared at him. I stared through the open door. Looked
down as far as down went, past the metal rim of the car into the
puddle right below it, to a small hollow, cloudy water, tiny rocks
embedded in the soil beneath. My shoes would get wet, my skirt
stained.

"Does it matter?" Walid asked me.

"Of course not." I unzipped the top of the backpack and slid
out my purse. "I almost forgot this—it's not like it's something
you'd need. Busfare and a note for my aunt and my identity card.
That's all."

"Good-bye, Nadia," Walid said. "Go in peace. Go with God."

"Good-bye."

"Nine o'clock tomorrow. God willing."

"God willing."

I was standing in the mud then, shoes dirty, skirt spattered.
The car pulled away from the curb gently, gained a little speed,
and roared off into the distance. Dark blue, a sedan of some sort,
the license plate covered with mud.

Swinging my purse over my shoulder, I pulled my feet out of
the puddle and crossed the street.

# In the Name of God,
# the Most Glorious One

It is very strange to wake up on the last day of your life. Oddly enough, I had overslept. Mama came in. "Nadia," she said. "You're going to be late for school." She had a kerchief on her head, as though she'd been going on and off the balcony, and my first thought was, she's been up for hours, cleaning in the early-morning cool.

My second: Today's the day.

I climbed out of bed. No grogginess or stealing extra sleep on my day of martyrdom. As I whipped into the bathroom, the phone rang and a male voice told the caller "Good morning." Nassir, sounding less in despair and more like his old self. Had I dreamed that scene in the moonlight? I looked down at my toes, still scratched and cracked where I'd scraped them against the cement balcony. Not a dream.

I flipped both taps and watched the lukewarm water tumble into the plastic bucket beneath. Shuddering a little, I washed myself top to bottom, including my hair. Paradise or the other place, at least I would be clean. Fully covered in robe and towel, I scooted back to my room where I dressed quickly and said my prayers. Late for morning prayer on my final day. Still, I prayed with a sincerity I seldom have. *There is no God but God, there is no God but God. Mohammad, Prophet of God. Come to the prayer. . . . There is no God but God. No God but God. But God. God.*

I wore my fancy white underwear with the ribbons, my favorite blue skirt, and the only silk blouse I own. Mama came in the room as I was fingering the thin, old-fashioned bracelets my father's mother had left me. Not expensive like the crescent necklace, but they might be worth something. "You're not wearing those to school?" she asked. "Nadia, I mean it that you're going to be late."

"I'm hurrying. Mama, you know, if anything happened to me, you could sell my things?"

Mama stopped in the bedroom doorway, broom angled outward like a weapon. "If anything happened to you? What on earth are you talking about?"

"A car accident or, or anything. I don't know."

She started sweeping the floor. "Nadia, you will be the death of me. I mean it. Is there something you want to tell me?"

*I love you. Be proud of me. This is for all of us.* I had skirted too close to the edge, though. Too much sentiment and she'd keep me home. I went cold at the thought of disappointing Walid, letting down God. Even though—was Walid married? It could have been the driver's joke. Not that it mattered. My decision had nothing to do with Walid, nothing at all.

I tied my hair back and stuck bobby pins in the strands that might otherwise stray. Leaving the room, I found the rest of the house in chaos. Dimah and Mariam had arrived to spend the morning with their father, and they shed mini backpacks and shoes as they ran into the salon. Mohammad sat on the couch, fending off their greeting with an ineffective hand while using the other to press the phone tight against his ear. "How hard can it be? I learned English, right? . . . No, don't tell them I'm willing to learn Dutch. Tell them I already speak it."

He glared at Dimah as she crawled up beside him and tried to push him off the couch, reaching for some bright plastic toy behind him. "What? Say I really like languages and I learned it from a tape. Then if I get the job, I *will* learn it from a tape." His raised forearm foiled Dimah, but Mariam wriggled in behind him and emerged triumphant with a plastic hammer. "Fine. Whatever you have to say. Just get me an interview. I'll go anywhere, as long as I don't have to stay in this godforsaken rat hole of a country."

I walked into the kitchen, where Mama and Nassir, heads bent together, were engaged in a secret conversation. ". . . I'll manage to get Mohammad's best tie, don't worry about that. . . ." Whisper, whisper. "Meet with them, and see if you suit each other. . . ."

"Meet with who?" Loud in the hushed kitchen, my words made them both jump. "The mother of your future bride?"

The stain on Nassir's skin started at his neck and flowed upward. "If you must know, I have a job interview. Management." Mama turned aside to cut the gas on the stove. "I'll be, um, managing accounts. If I get the job."

I stared at him. "Another interview?" He had no shame. "How nice to see that your connections are coming through for you."

Nassir's face looked like a tomato with a shock of black hair. In a voice that wavered between defiance and apology, he said, "I didn't get this through connections, Nadia. Someone actually read my resume online and called me."

I reached across Mama, took the kettle off the stove, and began pouring tea into one of the empty glasses set out on the counter. Some of the water slopped onto my fingers, scalding me. What difference did Nassir's conniving make, especially today? My mind should be occupied with purer thoughts on this *jihad* morning. After all, he would answer to God, not to me. I contented myself with one outraged look, and he had the decency to bow his head. "Nadia," said Mama, "I mean it, you're going to be late today. I've never seen you so slow."

I gulped my tea, wishing I could savor its sweetness. Like the morning, like life, it was gone too quickly. "I'm leaving now, Mama," I told her. I moved through the kitchen and into the hallway, pulled on my *manteau*, slid into flats. Time to go. Still, my reluctant feet stayed put inside the door. I could give it all up. After all, wasn't that what they were expecting me to do? The driver from last night and Walid's friends, whoever they were. Walid himself, maybe. I could stay here, study for exams, say my prayers, be a proper Muslim in the traditional way.

Walid, Walid's friends, they were irrelevant. What did God expect me to do?

It was Mama who decided it. "Get a move on, Nadia," she said. I leaned in through the kitchen and kissed her on both cheeks—kerchief, broom, and all. "I love you," I said, and it seemed appropriate. A kind of apology, she probably thought, for being so slow. "'Bye Mohammad, 'bye Dimah, 'bye Mariam," I shouted around the corner to the brother and nieces I couldn't see. And "Good-bye, Nassir," to the brother still in the kitchen. He looked surprised, but God is the only judge.

Then I was through the door and free of my family, until the Day of Judgment.

I let the hot sun warm my mind and my heart. Time to prepare myself for the final hour. Was I actually going to do this? With thoughts about my brothers and marriage and tea roaming through my head? *Calm down, Nadia. You have time to think, time to pray* duas. *Our Lord! Forgive us our sins and the lack of moderation in our doings, and make firm our steps and succor us against those who deny the truth.*

Deny the truth. Was that what I was doing? The truth was all around me: blue sky, happy sun, long strands of grass waving with the breeze. Was killing myself, for whatever cause, denying that?

*Deep breath, Nadia.* Duas, *not doubts. Our Lord! In You we have placed our trust, and to You do we turn in repentance, for unto You is the end of all journeys.*

This was my last journey, the last time I would feel the sun bear down on my covered head. Hot sun, hot pavement, hot as hell. *Breathe, Nadia.* I was doing the right thing, the Islamic thing. American feet marching into Baghdad, American mouths claiming the moral victory. Israeli grenades, launched with American dollars at innocent Palestinian babies. The only thing they listened to was death—just their luck, that was the only music I could play.

God was calling me. I could hear the drumbeat over and

above the snarl of traffic, the honking horns, the loud music that poured out of one car after another. The triumph of trumpets, the pounding march of righteous feet. *On that day they will follow the Caller: no crookedness can they show him: all sounds shall humble themselves in the presence of God most gracious: nothing shall you hear but the tramp of their feet as they march.* Step, step, right, left, step, step. That was me, feet in tandem with the call of God.

*God is great, God is great.* All my life, I'd wanted to put God ahead of everything else. Here was my opportunity to be the person he'd planned me to be. No more petty sins, missed prayers, idle gossip, jealousy. . . .

First of all, I wasn't jealous of her. Walid's wife. No, first of all, if he even had a wife—the whole thing could have been a joke, could have been the driver's way of testing me. Was I in this for God or for Walid? Second, if he *did* have a wife, what did it matter? In Islam, a man could take a second wife or a third or a fourth. The Qur'an said so, and the Qur'an said nothing backward or unjust, whatever impertinent Unbelievers might think. Funny that they took such issue with a man having a legal second wife, when they had marital relations with every girl they met on the corner.

Of course, Walid could have four wives already and it wouldn't matter to me. I had dedicated my life to God, and I was committed to living that promise in a very public way. It didn't matter to me if Walid had a hundred wives. Well, yes, it would because more than four was forbidden by Islam. Then again, that was between God and Walid. My concern was God and me.

Duas, *Nadia.* Duas. *O God, on this day, grant me the obedience of the humble, expand my chest through the repentance of the humble, by Your security, O shelter of the fearful.* Was I fearful? I was shaking in my sensible flats at the thought of facing God on Judgment Day. That was part of being a Muslim. God's power, His omnipotence, His truth, His justice, all shone with a brilliance that would hurt mere human souls. After death, anything could happen. I wasn't fool enough to think that martyrdom would earn me entry into heaven—only God decided, only God knew. And what would heaven be like? Not what I knew on Earth, not a chaotic salon and a kitchen overflowing with dishes, and math lessons that never finished. Not that.

Central Bank of Syria loomed before me. 8:57. *No loitering.* I slowed my steps, counting them. Fifty-one, fifty-two, fifty-three. . . I crossed the street and stepped up on the curb in front of the bank's open gate at the same moment that a dark blue car slid into the parking space beside me. My hands trembled so hard I curled them into fists. The door popped open. I took a deep breath, stepped inside to meet my fate.

"Peace be with you, sister."

I had expected the car wouldn't come. It would come, but Walid would not be inside. Walid would be there but would tell me he'd changed his mind. *Go home and play with your dolls, little girl. You didn't really believe that we would let you do something important, did you?*

I hadn't expected this—the car, Walid, his faith in me. My throat went dry and scaly as I made out a black bag, my backpack, in the backseat, a large lump visible inside its sealed zipper. Walid looked handsome in a pair of black pants and a bright blue shirt, open at the neck, black shoes, black socks, worried frown. The driver—same black cap pulled low over his eyes—was a different man, older, with a grizzled neck and graying hair.

"And peace be with you."

We drove along for a moment, down one small street and then another. Walid stared at the back of the seat in front of him. "Are you sure about this?"

I was. A rush of something flooded through me. In a few minutes, no more than an hour, I'd *know* what people wonder their whole lives. Had I done well enough, had I succeeded in God's plan for me? To some extent I knew already. "I'm sure." My voice sounded confident. "It's meant to be me."

"Are you doing this for Fowzi?"

It was for Fowzi. And for all the other Fowzis who'd been arrested after doing nothing worse than speaking their minds. And all the millions of almost-Fowzis who'd kept their mouths shut, censored themselves, been held back from saying what they really meant. I held the next thought close to me for a second before I let myself think it. This mission was for Nassir, too, and all the other men and women with their backs pressed against the wall by poverty and despair. Nassir, his life ruined just as surely, just as thoroughly as Fowzi's ever was.

"That's between me and God," I said. By the time the words came out, the car was rounding a corner and Walid had leaned over and removed a rectangular brown case from my backpack. "Strap it around your waist," he instructed me. "Then carefully run this wire up your side and along your arm. When you're ready, not one minute, not one second before, you pull this tiny lever." He showed me how it worked, once, twice, three times, and made me repeat the simple instructions back to him. Once, twice, three times. I took the—yes, the bomb—took it with stiff fingers, rested it beside me on the seat. *Not a toy.* Walid turned his head while I slid out of my *manteau* and attached the heavy case around my waist, aligned the thin wire up my side, ran it down the length of my arm. Secured it into place around my wrist. Heavy, it jingled when I moved. "Don't worry," he said. "It can't go off by accident. You have to press the lever."

I nodded. I pushed my awkward, frightened arms back inside my sleeves and secured my *manteau* over my shoulders. I buttoned it all the way to the top.

"Are you ready?"

"I'm ready."

"Drive down to Maysaloun Street," he told the driver. "Pull up on the corner." The driver, mouth closed tight and grim, swerved left. Walid turned and looked me in the eye. "Walk straight up the street, as casual as you can, as though you're going to meet friends. Step inside Hotel Cham and turn right, walk straight ahead until you reach the gift shop. Peer into the glass window, but try to look impatient, as though you're waiting for someone. Foreign tourists will be swarming all over the lobby. Wait for the most opportune group to approach. We want to make this story as nasty as possible, get the whole world's attention."

His eyes shone with something. Righteousness? Excitement? I couldn't look away. "Don't pull the switch before nine thirty. After that, as soon as possible. Don't wait more than five minutes— longer than that, and the security guards might get suspicious."

I swallowed. "Will there be Muslims there too?"

"If they're righteous Muslims, they'll go to heaven. As martyrs, sacrificing their lives for the sake of the community. If not, well, that's their own mistake; they should have been." He tapped his fingers on his left knee. "Are you backing out?"

The car weaved into the traffic that clogged the roundabout then pulled to the edge of Maysaloun Street, but did not stop. "Of course not," I said.

"Of course not. Give thanks to God. Nadia . . . ."

"Yes?"

"Can I keep your bag? As a reminder of you? It wouldn't be right to ask for anything else, not a handshake, not even a look, certainly not a kiss. But your bag—well, I'd like to remember you."

I was surprised, more than surprised, warmed. "Of course."

"Your family will be well looked after," he said. "Don't worry."

"I know they will," I said. "God looks after those who obey His commands." I opened the door and climbed out of the car, moving my left arm as little as possible. "Good-bye, Walid."

"Go with God, Nadia."

I went. With God at my side and by my heels and carrying my back, I walked the one hundred yards to Hotel Cham, the fifty yards remaining, the twenty-five, the ten. Casual yet confident. I heard the blue car speed away behind me, the last I would ever see of Walid on this, the last day of my life, and I didn't care. *Are you prepared to meet your Maker, Nadia?*

A simple question. I closed my eyes, said my prayers. *God is greatest, God is greatest.*

Yes. I was prepared.

I walked through the revolving doors, stumbled as the person on the other side walked just a little faster than I did. A man, with a business suit and briefcase slung over one arm. I tripped and fell into the door, caught myself against the glass with the broad of my forearm. Held still for the blast and then—my right arm. I'd balanced myself with my right arm.

The cool air inside the door caught me off guard. I'd seen Hotel Cham a million times, driven past it, but I'd never been inside. Fancy tiles lined the floor, sumptuous armchairs dotted the lobby, clear-as-diamond water tinkled against the stones on the bottom of a large fountain. Breathtaking. But I didn't have time for that. I stood, just one minute, in the doorway, and let my eyes wander the room.

I took the sharpest right and, ten paces ahead, found the gift shop Walid had promised would be there. The shelves in the window were lined with traditional crafts: inlaid chess boards, handblown hubble-bubble pipes, ceramic coffee sets. On the other side of the lobby, behind the reception desk with its suit-and-tied hotel workers, a clock ticked off the minutes. 9:29.

9:30.

I looked over my shoulder. Behind me, a pair of leather armchairs offered comfort to weary travelers, but their high backs made it impossible to see whether they were empty or occupied. Beyond the chairs, a group of northern Europeans with long legs and pink faces bent their heads over an open map. Half a dozen Japanese tourists, necks weighed down with cameras, poured out of the elevator. A family of Gulf Arabs stood in the corner, a young girl about my age fiddling with her black veil.

Americans. I wanted Americans. A group of old people

emerged from the gift shop, their hands full of wrapped packages. They were speaking English. Were they swallowing the ends of their words? I moved closer, inclined my head. "This Pharaoh's bust is the very thing Janice would pick up if she were here," one woman said, her soft white hair bobbed at her neck. "I know exactly what she'll say, too: 'Mom,' she'll say, 'you don't have to go to these outlandish places to buy something you could have ordered online.'"

Americans. I edged along the glass window, close enough to touch Janice's mother. *Allahu Akbar, La illaha il Allah*—

A hand jolted my elbow. "Nadia?"

I whirled around.

"What on earth are you doing here? Aren't you supposed to be in school?"

"What am I doing here? What are you doing here?" Nassir. In pressed pants and a white shirt, the blue silk tie Mohammad had brought back from the Gulf. Black shoes shined so heartily the gift shop sign winked in them. A moment later the shoes caught Nassir's frown. He tugged at his collar and his face took on the same shade of red it wore the last time I saw him. The last time I thought I'd ever see him.

"I have my job interview this morning, remember? If I get it, I'll be working here. I'm supposed to meet the interviewer over there." His right hand gestured at the high-backed chairs behind me. "*Don't be even a minute late*, they told me." He scowled . . . . "But here it is, nine thirty-two, and no one's shown up yet."

One moment. I had one moment. After that, Nassir would be pushing me through the door, hailing a taxi to send me back to school. *Press the lever, Nadia.* Raise high the green flag of the Prophet. Strike a blow for Islam. Invigorate and unite Muslims everywhere. And kill my brother? It was a sign, it had to be, but a sign of what? Green light—Nassir's betrayal represents the ultimate evil, warranting destruction on the grandest scale? Or red light—it's never acceptable to kill your own brother, no matter what he's done?

"Fine," said Nassir, sounding like he was standing much farther than two feet away. "It's not exactly a management position. But I didn't lie, I'll be managing the accounts of people who check in here, with the hotel. As a receptionist." His voice grew more defensive with every word. "But it's going to lead to something more. The man who called me, he said he was interested in my skills, my credentials; he was willing to take a chance on my potential. It's an entry-level job, but this is a big company. If I do well here, they'll find me a position in my field. Something that might even change the world, he said. A bit grandiose, but there you have it."

I stared at him.

"Normally I wouldn't take this kind of job, but after everything . . . well, you know, Nad. You're the only one who does. The thing is, this guy was very persuasive, and something he said . . . ." He had my full attention now. "What was it? Oh, yes, 'your time has come.'"

A coincidence? It had to be. But of their own volition, my memories rearranged themselves. The story they were telling wasn't the story I had lived. I clung to the words and phrases I remembered, to what I thought we'd said. Walid might be angry at Nassir's betrayal, but he'd never arrange for my pious sacrifice to destroy my own brother.

The puzzle wheel shifted again. Black cloak replaced the gauzy robes, horns the halo. Had I betrayed Nassir the same way he'd betrayed Fowzi? *You didn't think we'd just let it go, did you, Nadia?* I'd heard the words, understood them. Yet I'd gone on to tell Nassir's story, letting anger warp my judgment, just as Nassir had let desperation overwhelm his.

"Nadia? Are you listening to me?" Nassir took a step back. I couldn't see what he must have taken in—flushed cheeks, sparkling eyes, fear, uncertainty—but I could imagine it. "You're here to meet a boy, aren't you?"

"No," I said. Even to my own ears, this sounded like a lie.

*It's God that matters, Nadia, not Walid. Can't you set his manip-ulations to the side, continue down the path to glory on your own?* I raised my right hand to my left wrist, slipped it inside the loose sleeve of my *manteau*. Braced myself for one unendurable mo-ment. Then I touched the wire that linked the bomb to the explo-sive device, twisted, and disconnected it.

No. I couldn't push Walid to the side. The faintest smell of his cologne still lingered, the echo of his final words sounded in my ears. How I'd admired his faith, his single-mindedness. Now I could hardly bear to think about him, I couldn't stop. Whatever I might think of his tactics, didn't Walid love God with sincerity, worship Him, yearn to give his life for Islam? But it wasn't Walid standing in Hotel Cham, a bomb strapped to his waist.

And suddenly I couldn't think of a single kind thing Walid had done. He'd argued, fumed, thundered—been outraged over the Muslim who'd cheated the old lady in the grocery. Yet when a different shopkeeper, stick in hand, chased a boy out of his shop, had Walid stormed across the street, chastised the shopkeeper, given the hungry boy money for food? No. He'd stood on the corner, plotting with me. Was I guilty of the same charges I lev-eled against the glamour girls who panted after Western boys with their tight jeans and guitars? In love with an image, not a person? All the missteps I'd taken, all the miscalculations I'd made—had I been walking a crooked path from the beginning? Bassam, cast as villain X, when his only crime was to disagree with me. Nassir, prayers said and charity given, quietly going about the business of putting his cousin in prison. Had Mama been right all along? Following a set of rules, condemning others for stepping out of line, is not enough. Religion requires a person to stretch herself with kindness, to make allowances, to seek out good in everyone.

My judgment, once so crystal clear, now so suspect, I didn't trust at all.

I clutched my fists hard enough that my nails dug deep into

the skin of my palms. Would any plot to destroy part of God's creation always include corrupt twists and turns? I didn't know. I knew only that there would be no glorious explosion today, no change of history's course, only a little girl who'd behaved like an irresponsible teenager.

I let Nassir shepherd me to the revolving door. His smug lecture grew louder and more intelligible. I was sinking back into my own skin, worrying about the homework I hadn't finished, dreading the look on Mama's face when Nassir marched me through the front door. The moment, my moment, had come and gone.

I felt the glass against my arm again, this time a cold, sharp symbol of a world I couldn't reach, and then I was outside, blinking hard in the bright sunlight.

PAULA JOLIN